Acclaim for *Let the Lion E* W9-CGK-201

"Ellease Southerland's own dreams and memories, as well as her literary style, are imbued with African folklore, making her story seem less a novel than a myth."
                                                                —*New Yorker*

"Like a finely wrought poem, *Let the Lion Eat Straw* deserves more than one reading. . . . It is reminiscent of works by Maya Angelou, by Anne Moody, by Toni Morrison. . . . It is a story that sticks in and haunts the shadowy places of one's mind . . . that transcends race and class. . . . Southerland has written a remarkable first novel."
                                                                —*Los Angeles Times*

"Lovely. . . . Exquisitely rendered in an almost musical cadence that fits the story perfectly. It approaches the level of myth."
                                                                —*Boston Sunday Globe*

"There is more life and character, more that will linger in the mind, than in countless novels twice as long."   —*New York Post*

"A masterpiece . . . brilliant, graceful, poetic!"
                                                                —*St. Louis Post-Dispatch*

"The kind of book which makes the reviewer sort through his arsenal of adjectives and recognize with pleasure that 'beautiful' hasn't outlived its usefulness. . . . Powerful human truths."   —*Newsday*

"A warm, loving homage . . . an effective blend of naturalistic detail shaded with a suggestion of the mystical . . . an accessible, involving drama that illuminates the Afro-American experience."
                                                                —*Chicago Tribune Book World*

"Tangible, breathing life. . . . It's difficult to believe that a first novel can be at once so finely honed and so rich of characterization and action. But this one is."   —*Chattanooga Times*

"This book is a miracle. . . . As a debut it is astounding; as an achievement it is even more so." —*Sunday Times* (London)

"Ellease Southerland is a seer of the interior human landscape. In *Let the Lion Eat Straw*, she gives her vision to her readers. I, for one, am grateful. Ellease Southerland is welcome. Ellease Southerland is a joy." —Maya Angelou

"Strong and beautiful. . . . There is so much courage, honesty, and life in this novel."
—Shirley Hazzard, author of the National Book Award winner *The Great Fire*

"Important. . . . It has a rich, live, radiant validity, offering characters memorably exciting." —Gwendolyn Brooks

"Beautiful. . . . Southerland is a major literary talent. . . . A talent which transcends race and color, and touches the universal. This is indeed a love story for everybody." —Madeleine L'Engle

"A beautiful book . . . of startling originality, simplicity, insight, and grace." —Richard Elman

"Fresh, original. . . . It's fine reading." —*Detroit News*

"A lyrical, emotive odyssey. . . . This rich first novel sings on the page." —*Kirkus Reviews* (starred)

"With words that seem to sing . . . *Let the Lion Eat Straw* will make you laugh and cry." —*Columbus Sunday Dispatch*

"A sensitive, strong evocation of a life and of commitments made and honored." —*Publishers Weekly*

AMISTAD *An Imprint of* HarperCollins*Publishers*

Let
the Lion
Eat Straw

ebele oseye

(Ellease Southerland)

Originally published in 1979 by Charles Scribner's Sons.

FIRST AMISTAD PAPERBACK EDITION PUBLISHED 2005

Book design by Shubhani Sarkar

Printed on acid-free paper

The Library of Congress has cataloged the hardcover edition as follows:

Oseye, Ebele.
Let the lion eat straw / Ebele Oseye.— 1st Amistad ed.
p. cm.
ISBN 0-06-072420-X (alk. paper)
1. Brooklyn (New York, N.Y.)—Fiction. 2. African American girls—Fiction.
3. African American women—Fiction. 4. Migration, Internal—Fiction.
5. Birthmothers—Fiction. I. Title.

PS3569.O765L48 2004   2003065386

813'.54—dc22   ISBN 0-06-072421-8 (pbk.)

05 06 07 08 09 BVG/RRD 10 9 8 7 6 5 4 3 2 1

For
> Yawaridi
> Takwa Fida
> Ahomeka
> Meliedike

Four who stood in close circle during the storm and hugged each time the thunder struck.

And
for
> Earthel

The wolf also shall dwell with the lamb, and the leopard shall lie down with the kid; and the calf and the young lion and the fatling together; and a little child shall lead them.

And the cow and the bear shall feed; their young ones shall lie down together; and the lion shall eat straw like the ox.

Isaiah 11:6–7

Let

the Lion

Eat Straw

1   Jackson didn't have good sense. He had all the sense he was born with, but that wasn't enough. He was a great big boy, sixteen years old and what'd he do all day? Go on up the road to the midwife's place and play just as content with the little girl there. Playing tea party. That ain't no way for a grown boy to be. Just two years ago, the little girl fix mud cakes and all. Took weeds and fixed it sos it looked like greens and laid a twig beside the dinner for a fork then called Jackson to the table to eat and that great big boy picked up the little mud cakes and bit right into them. And Abeba Williams, that's the little girl, put her hand on her hip just as she see the midwife do and said, "Jackson, you to play eat, not to eat mud sure enough." And Jackson got it straight after that.

And Jackson quick to tell people, "Me and Abeba going to get married."

And people say, "Who's Abeba?" And come to find she somebody no more than a baby and he a big boy holding her hand. They called him crazy. Crazy Jack. Except for the little girl, the midwife and Jackson's family. And sometimes he get on his brother's nerves and he call him the same thing. Crazy Jack.

Jackson had just gone down the road to play with Abeba. Banged on the door. Door wasn't locked, just pushed to. He holler her name. "Abeba."

Folk said, he's feeling hisself and going to hurt that little girl one of these days.

"Abeba!"

Then he come on back home to worry his mother to death.

"Where Abeba?"

"I told you they went to town, Jackson. Calm yourself."

"She not home. I was just fixin to stop by but she not home."

His mother kept washing.

"She gone north?"

"Jackson, don't worry me today."

"Where she at? She gone north?"

"Not yet, Jackson."

"When she going?"

"At the end of summer."

"How come Abeba going north?"

"Her mother's coming for her. Jackson you been asking me the same questions since morning."

"When she be back?"

"Jackson, sit down."

"I'm fixing to go to Abeba's house and wait till she get back from town. Bye Ma."

She let him go.

He soon came back.

He sat quietly in the yard.

His mother looked at him. Big hulking shoulders. Abeba Williams. The little girl with the pretty wide nose. That was an unusual little girl. With good understanding. Of course folk say that when two people sleep with their heads together, they get the same dreams. And Abeba slept with the midwife. Dreamed the old woman's dreams. Quite naturally she know some old folks' secrets. But weren't they two people proud of each other. Didn't have much of nothing, staying out in that one-room shack. Nothing but a rooster and a handful of chickens and a cabbage in the yard.

Didn't have no outhouse. Did their business right in the bush. But they were a proud somebody. The midwife, half Indian, half African. You could see it in her face. All in the cheekbones. And couldn't she bring some babies into this world. She could look up in the sky on a bright day and tell new life on the way. She start down the road and come across some nervous somebody beating a path to her house.

She was an unusual woman. She and the little girl come to the church door, with the same walk, same way of studying you. And the people had to turn, and see who's that so proud of themselves. And smiling and fanning. She looked at her son. "They be back directly, Jackson. You help me peel potatoes and directly it'll be time for you to go see is Abeba and Mamma Habblesham back from town."

In town, the midwife and the little girl met first one acquaintance and then another making over the little girl going to leave her Mamma Habblesham and go off to the big city to live with her natural mother.

Sister Mildred said, "Why you going way off from your Mamma Habblesham?"

The little girl looked troubled. Didn't answer.

"Every time I break bread with Abeba, it's sweet. Lord knows I don't want this baby to go way from me. What I got to do, Abeba not here? But I got to give all that up now."

Others stopped. Spoke in close-teeth whispers to keep the conversation over her ears. So the mother found herself a husband in New York. Hope she'll be happy. They said things louder for the little girl to hear.

"Be a good girl, Abeba."

"Yes ma'am." A feeling came over her. It felt like the times

Mamma Habblesham sang about God. Going to move this wicked race and get some other people who had better manners to obey. And not fight. Mamma Habblesham sang in front of the big tin basin where she washed the blood from chickens. Pulled out the wet feathers, and burned them in the fire outside.

They went into a goods store and looked at nice soft material. Abeba was very quiet as the man unrolled, spread and cut the cloth.

Back home, the little girl looked at the midwife and said, "You declare you tired?"

"I sure do, Abeba. Your Mamma Habblesham sure do."

"And there was plenty folks in town today?"

"Hush your mouth."

They smiled at each other. Glad to be home. Mamma Habblesham said, "Go open the package."

Abeba worked at the tight knot for a quiet minute, then said, "I believe it's too much for me to handle."

Mamma Habblesham cut the string with a knife and together they pulled back the brown paper and uncovered the soft fabric. Spread the cloth. Soft gingham, white and green squares. Pretty bright cotton, soft violet. And blue. Dotted Swiss. So much new cloth in the old shack with its one horsehair mattress, kerosene lamp. Chipped basins and old chairs.

Abeba felt the cloth, feeling a stronger sense of the North where her mother lived. She had two mothers. She felt the edge of the cloth, vaguely aware of the noises of the birds and small animals outside. The rooster, who realized that the women had returned, jumped over the wire fence and walked up to the open door. He hesitated, thinking of coming in. Abeba said, "Mamma Habblesham, we going to make a dress for you and a dress for me?"

"No. This for you special for when your New York Mamma get here so's you have something decent to take when you go north."

"Can you come to the North?"

"Too cold in New York for an old lady."

"How cold is it?"

"So cold the children wear thick coats and shoes and so on."

"Oh. Not to be just going out with one dress?"

"Sometimes wear two, three dresses."

"Oh."

"But your New York Mamma'll have plenty dresses for you. And after while, it be summer and hot most like it is here. Course you won't have no pecan trees and peanuts growing. Cold weather kill all that . . . Go get your Mamma Habblesham some lemonade." She saw the little girl studying things too hard and changed the subject. "And after that we go stir up some bread and boiled peanuts."

Abeba carried the cup carefully, smiling at the mention of boiled peanuts. She pulled out the sack of peanuts and put many handfuls into a tin plate.

"That'll do."

And the two women sat sipping lemonade and shelling nuts until directly there was a pot boiling steamy hot and smelling of peanuts and the little house burst with contentment.

Night came and it was a tired Abeba who slept in Mamma Habblesham's arms. The few dishes had been washed up. The rooster put back in the yard, the water that was pumped in the morning and used all day for hands and face, for dishes, for clothes, was finally thrown away, and the kerosene lamp burned for less than half an hour, put out. Abeba clutched the midwife's soft, wrinkly body.

"Sleep now." Mamma's pretty little flower. She had given that name: Abeba. Flower. Grown in sandy North Carolina. She stroked the little girl, shoulders, back, hips. Rubbed her head and pressed it close to her. A beautiful baby. Pretty wide nose, full brown eyes, the exact brown, bright brown like her father's. Catch her Mamma's hand and walk on up the hill to see is the postman come. And don't fret whether he come or not because the main reason they walk on out is just to enjoy and take in the sun. See how the trees and all look mighty pretty. They stand by the road for a spell and after while a car come. Stirring up dust and making enough fuss to kill the devil. Abeba think that something and admired it so. Eyes brighten. Get just as round. Then she look up at her Mamma Habblesham and say, "That car putting up a fuss, Mamma Habblesham."

"You sure right, Abeba."

She wished she could keep the little girl. Raised her from the time she's two months. Spent most every day of her six years together. Got to give that up.

Abeba's hand flew up. She moaned.

"You Abeba, turn loose that dream and sleep." She shook her.

Abeba moaned. "You Mamma Habblesham?"

"Your Mamma Habblesham right here. Rest now."

But when Abeba closed her eyes, the dreams towed her under. The postman gave her a doll. From the North. With the head cracked. Jackson held his head because the doll's head was cracked. Said his head hurt. None of it seemed to make sense to her. Then it did . . . New York. She imagined it very new there. In the York. Her mother doing new things. Her dream islands were memories. Scattered lights in the dark. Brightest when her mother visited. She had two mothers. Her mother was very big and smelled like the North. And her hair was flat and shiny. She had big eyes. "Have you been a good girl Abeba?"

She couldn't speak to the big eyes.

Does she talk?

She talk good. Say hello to your New York Mamma . . . Outside, all the chickens jumped the fence. They followed the rooster and walked around quietly because it was dark and they didn't want to bump into things.

Abeba reached for the soft body of the midwife, and held her in her sleep. Where things were the deep green of late summer. She heard the blackbirds' caw-caw. Felt the hot sun on her toes, smiled up at her Mamma Habblesham and slept evenly for the rest of the night.

Once Mamma Habblesham felt Abeba hit an even sleep, she let her own thoughts go to the mother. Miss Angela Williams. Tried so hard to keep house in a world of unkept houses. She was a big little girl, not too proud of her looks. Took her wide mouth and broad shoulders after her Papa, and wished that she looked more like her Mamma. Never missed church service. Always right up under her mother, even after she hit the double numbers and into her twenties. Naturally she took it hard when her mother got the stroke. Two years on her back. Couldn't move nothing on the right side.

It wasn't two months after her mother died that she looked into Angela's face and something struck her. And she said, "You in a family way."

"No ma'am."

"Yes you are." She spoke quiet so folks wouldn't hear. "I can tell by your eyes."

Angela Williams. Crying. Shoulders jerking.

"Here. Here. I'll stand with you. Good a woman as your mother was her children won't want for nothing. Your time come, I'll be in the room with you."

And that was how Abeba came into the world. Eyes new with a touch of quiet tension. Little legs shaped like mother's. Wide ankles, wide feet. You could see the father all round the upper lip and in the tiny nose. And she was brownskin like the father. It was Robert-Lee's baby, but he had gone off, soon's he found out Angela expecting.

Next thing, Mamma Habblesham had the baby, and she telling folk Angela gone to New York to find a job settle down and send for the baby.

Five and a half years went by and Carolina didn't see much of Angela. Folks thought of them always together. Abeba and her Mamma Habblesham. Finally the change was going to come. The little girl who made the Carolina sand gold, who watched the yams and okra grow, who tried to shake the pecan trees, was going off, a long ways off.

There was a loud banging at the door. Both sleepers awoke abruptly, realizing that the sun had been up for some time, the rooster leading the chickens in raising a ruckus because they hadn't been fed.

For a moment the wham-wham-wham! startled them, then they realized that it was Jackson and it must be close to noon.

"Just a minute Jackson," Mamma Habblesham called.

She opened the door and the new day filled the world. Rooster poked his head past Jackson's leg.

"Morning Jackson."

"My Mamma told me come round here and see how you and Abeba doing."

Abeba looked at him. He had already said that he wanted to marry her. And when they grew up, they would. It seemed for the moment that all that fuss about going up north was play talk. And that she and Mamma Habblesham and Jackson and the rooster would live forever.

2 Late in August, her mother came.

"Go on, Abeba, say hello to your mother."

"Hu—hu . . ." She looked quickly at her mother who smelled like the North. Fought with her words. "Hell—hel . . . O! New—York—Mamma." She stomped her foot to force the words out.

"Well. When did she take to stammering?"

"Just when she's the least bit excited. Been thinking about going a long ways off. And having a daddy and all. And she's the least bit excited."

"You been a good girl, Abeba?" Voice so strong and deep.

"Yu—yu . . ."

"Don't stammer. Say it, Abeba." Her mother clapped her hands. "Say it. Thank Mamma Habblesham for being so good to you all these years."

She looked at the old, thin body, her eyes shining with fever and love.

"I know she love me."

Abeba caught Mamma Habblesham's hand, and the old woman picked her up and turned the conversation round.

"The Wilsons be by this afternoon. And Charlie Jones' children. Folks want to hear about the big city, streets paved with gold."

Angela said, "Not a bit of gold. You hear me? Streets paved with nothing but trolley tracks." And she threw her head back and laughed.

Soon there were so many people in the house and in the yard front and back and folks brought food until laughter filled the Carolina town. They admired the big city where all the folk had electric light. Even poor folk. Toilet in the house. Running water. They said it did seem like heaven, but just the same not to keep Abeba too long, because they didn't see how they would do without her.

While the folk came and talked, Abeba stared at her mother. The stout nose, shiny and black with a mole on one side. She had no idea how many hours of pinching had gone into "pointing" that nose. Energy poured from her words. Abeba was awed by this woman whose strength flashed, who worked ten hours a day, ironing at the laundry on Decatur Street. Clothes flashed down on the ironing board, wrinkled, hit with a swift hot iron, smooth in two, three strokes. The employers admired her, but never raised her pay.

From that thirty-five dollars a month, she sent eight to Carolina to keep food in her daughter's stomach. When her shoes were turned over, she couldn't buy new shoes. Had to spend money for the baby. Needed a new dress because she was going to sing a solo, had to do without. Money, money, money. And the father off somewhere sporting and then she found where he was living in New York, so interested in another woman who had lighter skin, longer hair. Mouth not so wide. The fire ate a direct path to the Carolinas. Abeba. She was not a little girl, but trouble, trouble. Brought death and hard times. Even her grandmother's death, before Abeba's birth, seemed in Angela's mind Abeba's fault. The pain was continuous, and she blamed Abeba for all pain. Her own guilt confused.

Abeba sensed and felt things which she could not understand. And if Mamma Habblesham hadn't kept up with her even though there was so much company, she would have gone into a bad state. Jackson came by and spoke, but sat uneasy as the company thinned and left Angela, Mamma Habblesham, Abeba and himself. Abeba began to hope that her mother's staying and not going right away meant that something had been changed and that she would stay after all.

But time came to go. To begin a long trip on a bumpy bus that would take dangerous curves, ride through the night and heat up like a can during the noon sun and speed along, dumping into her memory small towns, dried yards, folk sitting out front, back, sometimes white, sometimes black. Abeba's head pained, fluctuating between sharpened interest and exhaustion. She dozed in fear, snapping awake until her New York mother put her on her lap and stroked her legs tenderly. And seemingly with the weight of sleepless years, Abeba slept.

Finally in Brooklyn after three days of travel, Abeba half-trotted in order to keep up with her fast-stepping mother. Brooklyn, her mother called it. Seemed a funny kind of night with its street lights. So different from the pure black Carolina night. She wondered at the moody big bulbs that cast a tin silver glow in the heat. It might not be New York yet because the North was cold. Where folks wore thick coats and shoes. It was hot and noisy. She stepped with her New York mother into the tangle of evening voices. Men and boys filled the corners. They seemed to come up, as if developed and printed by the night. They stepped out of the way so that the woman and her daughter could pass. They laughed suddenly. Spat and talked loud. One of them kept saying "Wait-a-minute-wait-a-minute." Sometimes they jumped back and punched each other. Abeba watched. They smoked their cigarettes so tight into the edge that it seemed like they smoked the insides of their fingers.

Music. She heard and turned suddenly. Saw boys standing in a circle looking into each other's eyes singing serious as cats:

> *Hey-bob-a-ree-bob*
> *She's my baby.*
> *Hey-bob-a-ree-bob*
> *Don't mean maybe.*

They sang it some more, moving their shoulders and heads. Old women with high blood pressure walked by in run-down shoes seemed to know the song. Women carried shopping bags of bad fruit from the markets on Glenmore and Pitkin, bags wet-brown with the juice of rotting fruit. Understood the song. Little girls in badly cut skirts with unwashed skinny legs hopscotched on the sidewalk, kicking soda-pop tops. Cars came and honked added their music then drove away into another reality. All these folk seemed to command life, seemed impressive people to Abeba. Who couldn't see that they brought their chairs to the sidewalk because their apartments were dark and dry with age. Iceboxes ran dry and stank with warmth. And they? A backlog of blacks from the back load of southern buses.

"Our folks won't do," her mother said. "Lazy, lazy folks. Do nothing but sit out all night. Wake up twelve, one o'clock and make devilment. Idle hands is the devil's workshop. That's all our folks good for, make babies."

A sudden noise swallowed her mother's last words, noise that cut every nerve in Abeba's body, scattered men and boys in the street. The ground rumbled and Abeba shook as the red drilling noise trembled around her. Her mother picked her up and held her. When the noise quieted said, "Big old fire engines got to make plenty noise so folk'll move out the way. Engine mash 'em up. Got to put the fire out."

People returned to the streets.

"But when God sets this world on fire, ain't no fire engine do no more good. Burn up everything. Fire truck. Fireman and his hose. Everything. Everything."

Abeba hoped that God wouldn't do that soon. Burn up everything like her mother said. Her dolly with the cracked head even.

"Thank the Lord we're almost home."

Abeba hesitated. Was that a direct order? And how should she thank the Lord?

They turned corners into a quieter block, darker street. The song on Abeba's mind.

"Home just down the block."

"Yes ma'am." She spoke right up.

"I want you to say 'yes Mommie.' Leave that country talk for the South. You're in Brooklyn now."

Hey-bob-a-ree-bob.

Inside the third-floor apartment here were other things to trap her attention. Soft white soap in the bathroom, water clean and shining in the commode. She touched the smooth bowl gently, feeling the coolness and her mother hit her on the wrist.

"Wash your hands, Abeba. Hands nasty. Nasty hands."

Her mother rubbed her hand between her big hands and put soap on them and ran the water in the sink and dipped them. Abeba sat on the bowl and did her business, then she looked up as her mother pulled the wooden knob at the end of the chain. She jumped back. There was a swooshing noise, water dropped from sight then came up again and trembled. Then was shiny and still.

Her mother made her wash her hands again.

They sat down at a new table with a slippery top. Red-handled spoons and forks. Her mother put a cushion under her and tucked paper under her chin. Soon she saw big dishes with steam coming out. Wanted to eat some, but her head, a jumble with the Brooklyn night and three days' ride, dipped suddenly to the table and she slept.

"Abeba?"

She opened her eyes and saw the Lord looking at her. He had a black and gray moustache. No hair. She sensed the sun-up.

"Now you're awake," he said. "You were sleeping like a little angel."

And her eye caught space of a missing tooth in the side of his mouth. His face so close she could smell his face. Wondered at the turn of his nose. The pores in his skin. Tiny hairs coming out. Somehow that explained the fire engine. The red forks. She looked about her suddenly as she felt herself being lifted. Now she must be *up* North. She expected that it would be cold outside.

"A little girl to bless our home."

She touched his bushy moustache and soft lips.

"Daddy's little Abeba." Her New York Daddy. The Lord was her Daddy. Hey-bob. She took a deep breath.

"Good morning New York Daddy."

"Abeba!" He swung her around and around and she grabbed his neck.

"Come wash your hands and face, Abeba. Baby can't come to the table nasty." She followed her mother, wondering about her father. Trying to sort the many worlds. She thought she had dreamed of calling Mamma Habblesham. And while she slept, thought she was there.

Her mother combed her hair.

Abeba's hands rested on the knees that were larger and firmer than the old woman's.

"Keep still, Abeba."

At the table her father made eyes at her and called her a good little girl and buttered toast and gave her some and took large bites. And all day she thought about her father.

But he did not sleep with her when nights came. Like Mamma Habblesham did. And in the empty, new bed, with its soft sheets, she ached for Mamma Habblesham. Slept fitfully and finally awoke at three A.M. shouting "Mamma Habblesham." But Mamma Habblesham didn't say nothing. Just the gray sound of a trolley rolling down Rockaway Boulevard. Mamma Habblesham was dead.

3   For a long time the Brooklyn mornings were too quiet. There were no roosters and chickens. High on the third floor, the morning sun came through the windows wordlessly. For what seemed years, Abeba dressed in the mornings, had breakfast with her parents and then went upstairs with Mrs. Carrie and her small children while her parents went to work. She envied the other children on their way to school. Some went nicely, carried a book under one arm. Some went carelessly, pushed and last-tagged each other. Dropped books and laughed. Stooped to tie a shoelace. All of it looked like heaven from the third-floor window. But she couldn't go until she registered. She turned that word over. She hadn't registered in time and would have to wait for February. But it seemed that February would never come. She had copied her abc's in the notebook her father brought her. Practiced writing her name on every page. Abeba Lavoisier. Williams was her old name. She didn't need that name anymore. It seemed only fair that since she learned her new name she be allowed to be in a real school.

At last February came. She learned the secret behind the black iron fence, the tall stone walls. High windows laced with steel net. The big, dark basement with white circles painted on the black floors.

The long tables and the smell of vegetable soup as the women cooked for four hundred children. There were long corridors, as in a dream with a thousand doors, each door numbered. Room 126 the blue letters on her door. She watched her teacher, Mrs. Plotkin, a young woman with deep black hair. Who wore crisp blouses. Sometimes the bright sun outside shined in her face. Bright snow edged the window ledge. Other times were winter dull, with only the school lights to brighten the room filled with brown wooden desks, black inkwells, black children. Some days the light reminded her of Mamma Habblesham standing on the hill in the sun. And she wanted to say, "Mamma Habblesham, there sure is plenty books at the school." And Mamma Habblesham would say, "Hush your mouth." School lifted the weight of missing Mamma Habblesham. Abeba was satisfied and walked home proudly, holding her book.

It was the second week of the term when she was coming home. The snow on the ground was slippery and wet, so Abeba and her new friend Barbara walked carefully. As they stood at the corner, about to cross, a boy ran by and the next moment Abeba was on the ground, splashed wet, and surprised. She first thought it was an accident, but looked up to see the boy laughing, making a face.

Barbara helped her up. Helped her wipe the snow off her legs. Shook out her notebook. "Let's me and you beat him up tomorrow," Barbara said.

Abeba was wringing water from her mitten. "And I didn't even interfere with him."

"He thinks he's so smart. The basket. We'll knock the you-know-what out of him."

They walked together. Abeba shaken and glad to have her friend. Three blocks later they turned their separate ways.

When Abeba stepped into the house she was still trying to understand that evil boy when she heard her mother.

"Come home with your coat all dirty, stockings dirty and Mommie work too hard washing and ironing, working my fingers to the bone . . . Come this way, young lady."

When she followed her mother into the bedroom, she found herself grabbed, her mother whipping her legs with an ironing cord.

She put her hands out, trying to ward off the blows. Trying to get her mother to be more reasonable. She was briefly silent. Stunned. Then realized that the whipping would go on and on until she cried out. So she cried. Trying to understand why her mother's eyes flickered like darkened fire.

"Now go wash out those stockings and hang up that coat." Abeba went to the bathroom. Her head swimming, throat burning. She snapped the water on.

"And don't play with that water in there."

She washed the stockings. Laid them flat on the tub, then opened the closet door. Put herself behind the clothes, stuffed her mouth with a dress and, half-gagging, cried until she was exhausted. Then ripped a dress and sat there in the stuffy dark. At one moment her mother opened the closet door, then closed it again. Abeba didn't move until she heard her father's voice.

When he saw her, his voice dropped. "Angela, look at this child." He lifted her. Patted her head against his shoulder. "What happened to Daddy's little lady?" He splashed her face in cold water because her eyes were puffed and almost closed. Her head hot.

"Been sulking all afternoon because I gave her a little spanking."

"Why'd you spank her, Angela?"

"Come home wet, coat dirty. I send her out every morning looking decent."

"A boy in another class just pushed me down in the snow and

I didn't interfere with him." She started to cry again, wetting her father's neck and collar.

"Don't spank her, Angela."

"Arthur, that's my child."

"Don't spank her."

"She's got to mind. You spoil her rotten."

"I don't approve of you whipping her for nothing."

"I borned her!" There was fire in that statement. Anger and resentment.

And the husband was quiet.

The next day, a tall man visited Public School 84. At least he seemed tall to the children, with his trimmed moustache, sprinkled with gray hair. His coat was open at the neck, showed his black tie, bright clean white shirt. Abeba sat with the other students and proudly watched him. She could barely sit still.

"That's Abeba's father," Barbara whispered.

"That's your father?"

"Yes." She looked at the doorway where Mrs. Plotkin and her father talked. Mrs. Plotkin waved her over.

Abeba walked nicely, the class watching.

The three talked at the door, then Mrs. Plotkin called Barbara, who came, tucking in her blouse.

Those near the door picked up words. "His name is bad Oliver and he's in class 1-5. And we didn't do nothing to him."

"Who's his teacher?"

"Miss Abrams," the girls said together.

"Children," Mrs. Plotkin said, "there's to be no talking. I'm going down the hall with Mr. Lavoisier and I don't want to hear a sound." She gave them meaningful looks. But hadn't taken four steps before a din rose.

Mrs. Plotkin reappeared. "All right, children. Heads on desks.

And I don't want to hear a peep from you. Janet come to the front of the room."

Janet was a hefty little girl.

"If anyone lifts his head, let me know." She stood a moment. Then she left.

Heard Janet's voice. "Put your big head down, Clyde."

The four walked down the corridor to Mrs. Abrams' class. She was a white-haired teacher, so old that she didn't always get around to bad boys like Oliver.

The Abrams students sat very still as the teacher, parent and two students walked in.

The teachers talked, then Mrs. Abrams said, "Where is he?" Her voice was filled with age.

Barbara pointed him out.

Oliver looked frightened.

"That's the boy who pushed me down for nothing."

"Did not." He said that just for formality. He knew that he was accused and cornered. "Did not."

"Did too!" Barbara screamed.

"Come forward, Oliver." Mrs. Abrams picked up a ruler.

He came slowly.

"He was running so fast yesterday," Barbara said. Frowned bitterly with the total anger of a six-year-old.

The adults smiled to themselves. "Come on, Oliver."

The students watched carefully.

Mrs. Abrams stepped clumsily toward him. Showered blows on his shoulder. He moved and one bounced off his head.

The class called out.

Mrs. Plotkin thanked Mrs. Abrams and the group returned to class. "You have a lovely daughter, Mr. Lavoisier. Matter of fact we'll be putting her a grade ahead if she keeps up the good work."

"I'm mighty proud."

"And she gets along well with the other children. Oliver is one of the problem children. But I don't think she'll have any more trouble with him."

Abeba held her father's hand. Held Barbara's hand.

The father took them aside. "Some boys are mischievious," he said.

"What's mischievious?"

"They like to throw rocks at girls. Pull their hair or push them down. Sometimes they do it because they're playful."

"I don't want to play with rough Oliver."

"Me neither," Barbara said.

"When a boy is mischievious, you mustn't cry and run home. You must give them a punch."

The girls laughed.

"That's what my mother say. If anybody hit you, hit 'em back. And she say or else don't come home."

"Yes, you do have to hit them back. If you don't give them a good punch, and I mean a hard one, they'll push you every day at three o'clock. Understand me?"

"Yes Daddy."

And so, Abeba was ready for the next few years. Her composition, reading and math amazed her teachers. She was skipped twice. Teachers talked about her on their lunch hours. Abeba Lavoisier. Must be from one of the French-speaking islands. She was too different from those described as "our children." They gave her special smiles as she walked through the halls. Watched her head for home and spoke about her again when they reached their own houses.

Yet, Abeba heard nothing pleasant from her mother. It was her father who sat her on his knee each evening and looked at each page in her notebook.

"Spell 'come.' "

"Easy. C-o-m-e."

" 'Yesterday.' "

"Y-e-s-t-e-r-d-a-y."

"That was a long one. 'Table.' "

She spelled quickly. "T-a-b-l-e."

"Very nice." He turned a page. Looked seriously at a giraffe stamped at the top. "Why here's a giraffe!"

She laughed.

"Must have escaped from the zoo and jumped in your book. Is there a zoo in your book, little girl?"

"No, Daddy. It means it's nice neat work."

"Well, well, I thought it was a giraffe, but it really means nice neat work . . . And it is neat too."

She kissed him on his scratchy chin.

"How would Daddy's little flower like to go to the zoo and see the elephants?"

That Saturday was filled with echoes in the monkey house. One lion's roar. Slow-walking elephants. Thick-legged. Fancy birds squawking. Abeba astonishingly happy holding her father's hand, staring at the rumply stomach of the orang-utan, searching for his face. In her dreams no elephants would trample her. Because her father would snap their trunks.

So even if she stuttered in her mother's presence, the first two years with her father were joy.

Yet even her mother would bring new sunshine to Abeba's life.

One afternoon she called. Her voice warm and thoughtful. "Would you like to play an instrument?"

"Yes, Mommie."

"What would you like to play?"

"The piano."

"All right. Mommie's going to work hard to get your piano. And I don't want you to fool me now."

"Yes, Mommie."

Even as it was said, it was done. Three months later, there was a big truck on the streets to make a delivery. Abeba saw the truck way down the block as she and Barbara walked together.

"Look!"

Right before their eyes, the streets which were empty suddenly filled. The piano came. Black and shining in the May sun. Music for the people who prayed first for the Promised Land and settled for the projects. The piano came. People left cold houses and came out to see. Came from down the block and around the corner. Dogs stopped walking to watch the people. People dressed in fifty-cent coats. Thin shoes. The folk stood together on that pretty spring day staring at the instrument.

Angela stood passively nearby. Smiled. "Just ain't that something beautiful."

"Daggone! That thing is stone new, Jake. How much you think it cost?"

"Hundred dollars."

"More'n that!"

Abeba stood with Barbara. "Anybody could just play the piano if they want to. But not to break it up."

They shoved and begged. Mispronounced her name. "Hey, me play Abeba?"

"Sure."

"How about my brother?"

"He could."

"Abeba?"

"Yes, Mommie."

"I don't want these rough boys banging on the piano, please ma'am. Rough boys tear up everything. And Mommie and Daddy got to work, work, work to pay for this piano. And I don't want anybody in the house when I'm not home."

"Yes Mommie."

"And you boys don't ask her to play. Abeba's going to have lessons. You've got to have lessons. You've got to be taught before you can play the piano. Ask your mothers to teach you to play. Keep you busy and out of mischief. Idle hands is the devil's workshop."

The delivery men called to each other. "You got it Charlie?"

"Okay, Mike. Go ahead."

"Okay."

They told the people, "Stand back."

Mommie repeated, "Stand back. Back, back." She told the white man nearest her, "This my daughter's going to be a concert artist."

"That's nice, lady . . . Stand back."

"Who's going to be no concert artist?"

"She is."

"Who?"

"That girl right there with the ribbons."

"Oh. How old she?"

"How old you is?"

"I'm eight years old."

"You plays?"

"I'm going to have lessons."

"She don't never come out to play."

"Stand back."

"Supposing that thing fall on somebody. They be dead."

"They fixin to put it through the winda."

Commotion became stillness. Eyes watched the piano on a pulley roll in slow movement lifted to the third floor. Positioned several times then eased through the window where the frame had been removed.

"Well done," Angela said. "Well done, gentlemen. That's just lovely."

Inside, the piano was magnificent. And quiet. Its dark shiny surface reflected everything, the awe-struck Abeba. It smelled new. Each key so bright and firm, sensual in its firmness. It occupied the center of family thoughts. Sat grandly in dreams.

And soon a year passed with Abeba progressing from "finding middle C and all the other C's on the piano" to Hanon's *The Virtuoso Pianist in Sixty Exercises.* And her teacher praised her each Saturday when her father brought her for lessons.

"Daddy, a dot increases the value of a note by one-half!"

"Is that so? I thought a dot was a period. Or just a marking on the page by a careless person."

"No, Daddy."

"Or the mole on Miss Mildred's face."

"It's different in music."

"I see."

"Common time's the same as marching time."

He marched off.

"Come back, Daddy." She laughed.

They were going home, but stopped first at the five and dime, where her father bought her bright ribbons, socks, pencils. Some days. But every Saturday he bought her a root beer and a bag of peanuts.

"How many major scales are there?" she asked.

"Twelve." He answered promptly.

"Minor?" She sipped the root beer. Her eyes watered.

"Twelve."

Abeba smiled.

"And I'm twelve years old," her father said.

Abeba laughed. "Then you would be just a boy."

"Perhaps I am just a boy."

"Why do you have a moustache?"

"I must be a man."

She sighed. "Allegro?"

He answered quickly. "Fast."

"Adagio?"

He answered slowly. "Slow."

"Allegro moderato?"

He answered with medium speed. "Medium fast."

And when they left the warm smells of the store, she said, "Andante grazioso?"

He didn't say anything. Just walked "gracefully." Then held her hand and took the trolley home.

The empty beginner's page began to fill. Notes doubled. Full chords filled the staff. Change in time signature. Flags attached quickened the tempo. New notations. An eight trailing dots instructs one octave higher. Notes written below the staff like a planet dropped to distant space. Special lines had to be drawn to locate it. Abeba found those notes and a thousand tunes in between.

One Saturday her mother took her for lessons. There was no stopping on the way home. No talk. Her father wasn't feeling well. At home Abeba wiped the sweat from the trench in his upper lip, wiped his brow. He said quietly, "Can you play Handel's *Messiah* for me?"

She said, "I'm not up to that yet."

He was smiling at her seriousness. "How about 'Butterfly Etude'?"

She brightened. And soon the little apartment was filled with the quick-bright colors. The notes fluttered louder, then slower and very quiet. Pianissimo. The quiet-quiet flit of the butterfly.

And her father said that he had a touch of influenza, but the music made him better. And that he was fit as a fiddle.

And the next Saturday he was better.

Joy returned to the house. Abeba came each afternoon and filled the rooms with songs. Her mother listened. Washed. Faucets turned. Pots opened. Stirred. Closed. Oven. Her mother said, "That's a lovely piece." And sang in a strong contralto voice, sometimes getting ahead of the piano, then waiting. And sometimes she would stand at the piano and sing with her husband who had a high, twangy voice. It began to look like everything would be all right.

4   It was a Monday morning in September, shortly after Abeba's ninth birthday. She was getting ready for school when her mother called.

"Abeba."

She jumped. There was an urgent note in her mother's voice. Something about the morning quiet struck her.

"Come stand near your Daddy's bed."

She went into her parents' room. There were strange silences in that darkened place. A serenity weighted the dark tones of the bureau. Floor. She went to her father who was propped in a sitting position, touched his hand and held it. It felt cold. He breathed so carefully that her own breathing became careful. As she saw him more clearly, his face looked slightly ashy. His eyes shiny and tired. He didn't say anything at first. Then tried to talk and his teeth stuck to his upper lip. "Bring me a glass of water."

Her mother went for the water. He squeezed Abeba's hand long and hard. Except for his breathy sounds, lightly clearing his throat now and then, he was quiet.

Her mother brought the water and he released Abeba's hand to take the glass. He called them. "Abeba, Angela, put your hand on the glass."

They held the glass together.

He said, "Angela, give her a chance and she'll make it." Three

hands held the glass to his mouth and he drank until the glass was empty.

People came out of the morning, rushed into the room. Voices. Notes struck on the shining piano. Far from the corners of the block and across the street, people came. Abeba heard their footsteps reverberate on the stairs, rushing up the wooden flights. Three flights. A hundred. More. They came from the center of the earth running up a thousand years to see her father.

People spoke to the mother.

Children came. "Who done died?"

They were too loud. "Her daddy die."

Shush. The older women tried to make the children behave.

"Why he die?"

"I don't know."

Thin flocks of brown birds scattered through the day. Through the gray air in her head. Abeba sat on the tight sofa. Saw her mother moving. Talking softly. Being fanned and talked to. The women came to Abeba. Put their arms around her and kissed her on the head. She saw them from the distance hugging another part of herself. She was out someplace where there was no ground beneath her. It was the place way down yonder . . . where you couldn't hear nobody pray. Sometimes the lady said to her, "Your daddy was sure proud of you. And he's watching from heaven now, where he won't have no more pain."

One of her distant selves caught their tones and moods. The people seemed to have known for a long time about pain. About her father's pain. Her other selves just didn't know. There was the thin sweat. A quiet Saturday. Fit as a fiddle. And then death.

"Angela knew he had a condition before she married him."

"What condition? This is the first I'm hearing about it."

"Worked hisself to death."

"How old?"

"Fifty-seven."

"A young man."

"They say a young woman kills an older man. Angela just thirty-two you know."

The police came. Ambulance. Just white-covered him and took him away. The people were quiet and the woman held her. A woman like one in a dream whom you've never seen before but you recognize as though you've known all your life.

The little boy from upstairs, Mrs. Carrie's boy, just stood and sucked his thumb. Stared at her.

"He lived his life."

"Never had a mean word for nobody. I don't believe a cuss word ever passed his lips. And if anybody going to heaven, it's Arthur Lavoisier."

"He's with the Lord."

He is the Lord.

The women moved about making themselves useful. Some served the food they brought. Others pushed in chairs. Some checked the kitchen to start some cooking. Some kept the children from banging on the piano.

"And he been a good father to this child."

"Yes he has."

"Can't say that of every man. Many don't treat their own kids the way Arthur treated Angela's baby."

Voices lifted.

"Should Abeba wear a white dress or a black dress to her father's funeral?"

"How old you, baby?"

"Nine."

"Nine. Nine too young for black. She just a baby. Tell Sister Pearly Mae to sew up something white for this child."

Married four years. A shame. Just starting out together.

Four days later, the same faces came to the funeral. And more. The church seemed to have swung out its walls to hold all the sadness. Mesto. All the songs sung, slow sad songs, seemed to have a faster rhythm beneath them. The other song that replayed in Abeba's head:

> *Hey-bob-a-ree-bob*
> *She's my baby.*
> *Hey-bob-a-ree-bob*
> *Don't mean maybe.*

She was her father's baby.

5   First Angela sold Abeba's bed.
"Where will I sleep?"

Angela ignored her.

She slept in the big bed. With Angela.

Then she sold the bureau. Boxes of clothes. Dishes. The house echoed. Empty.

Wednesday afternoon, the piano! Roped. A hook dangled outside the window. Window frame removed.

Someone outside hollered up. "Okay."

Piano squeezed through the window. Disappeared.

"Come on," Angela said.

"Where?"

"Don't try my patience today."

They came to a cluttered street of battered, narrow walks. Stone Avenue. Filled with sounds. Hammerings. Skates nailed to long sticks. Wooden boxes. Her mother, wordless, stepped through the children.

Neighbors shouting.

"You boys get off that roof!"

"You not my mother."

"Children today so fresh."

Abeba stepped through the nails laid out on sidewalks. Wooden boxes. Soda caps lined up to decorate homemade scooters. She and her mother quiet.

"They dig up the sewer grate. Bust bottle. Smoke before they hit the double numbers."

"Thirty-three," Angela mumbled.

They went into the building. Abeba's eyes stretched in the darkness. Paper black. Wet smelling. Like the soft bottom of the ocean.

"Mommie! I can't see."

"Jesus, help me with this difficult child!"

She stumbled close to her mother. Walked up twisting stairs. Around corners. Up deeper into the dark. Stumbled. There was talking around her in rooms. Her mind rolled and pitched.

Up more steps.

Angela stopped.

Abeba waited for her knock. Surprised; she took out a key. Opened the door.

The piano! Sitting under a half-window. Bed squeezed close to the wall. Table. Chairs.

Perhaps her own bed was in another room.

"Bathroom in hall," Angela said.

Abeba hesitated. Saw Angela's eyes. Vanished. Felt along the wall. Found a door.

The toilet was soiled. Wet and cold. Seat splattered with dry paint. She closed the door. Sat. Jump up. Crack bit her soft thigh.

Faint sun came through the small gray window. Outlined a fresh chicken, killed, hung upside down.

Abeba screamed. Saw the blood dripping, the thick eye closed, and screamed until Angela rushed in. Held her.

Abeba in bed alone these autumn nights. Her face near the hard walls. Awoke in soft ropey dark. Heard rats.

"Meow!"

Wanted them to think she was a cat. Half-slept until her mother got home. Midnight.

Saturday morning. Bright December morning. Abeba awoke. Half-dreamed her father squeezed a tall tree through the door. Brushed the weather off himself. Admired the tree from Flatbush. Full and fresh. Abeba stretched her eyes wide in the tiny room. Her father was dead.

Through the wall, Abeba heard Irene talking to her baby. Irene was fifteen. The idea tiptoed around in Abeba's mind. She listened to the soft whimpering sounds that broke into a full cry.

Flatbush. She would help her mother carry the tree.

"Grown men and women come to the bathroom, put some in the bowl, put some on the floor."

Angela cleaned the hall toilet.

"Lord have mercy, this bathroom stink. Stay stink. Stink folks." She scrubbed. Talked. "Big strapping menfolk lazy and dirty. Sit around all day all night. Sleep half the morning, making mischief. Our folks good for nothing but making babies."

Abeba listened.

"Got to take my few pennies. Buy enough CN to clean out this place. Lord have mercy. Have mercy Jesus. Work all week till twelve midnight. Use up my few pennies . . ."

Suddenly she was in the room.

Abeba sprang from the bed. Tried to stay from underfoot as Angela pulled the sheets tight. Spread and tucked covers. Stepped on Abeba. Then fussed.

"So slow. Slow as a old woman."

Abeba stood between foot of bed and closet. Rubbed her foot. Pulled off flannel gown. Put on undershirt. Pink snuggies.

Angela stood near the oil heater, warmed a pot of milk.

"Where's your cup?"

Abeba held her cup. Drank flat warm milk. Watched her mother over the rim. Her whole body listened to the thin tune Angela hummed. Absent-minded.

Quiet.

Angela studied her plump legs. Ankles. Feet.

"Abeba?"

"Yes, Mommie."

"Wax the floor for me."

"Yes, Mommie."

"Then put a few clothes in a shopping bag. Go spend Christmas with your father. Mommie's broke. Funeral took all Mommie's money."

"My father!" She whispered in a baffled voice that begged Angela to be merciful. "Daddy's dead."

"That was not your daddy!" Her mother's eyes stretched strange. Tumbled anger.

Cold water beat the empty metal bucket. Abeba turned the faucet. Her hands numb. Lugged the bucket, splashed water through the hall. Into the room. Her body yanked and jerked.

"Don't try me this morning, Abeba."

Sharp daylight burned every street. Abeba stumbled on the steps, her "father's" steps.

"This where your daddy live. Done nothing for you but here just the same."

Thick ivy curled through iron. Sunshine on winter green leaf. Willoughby Street. Deep inside the house the bell ringing.

Grave-soft footsteps. Her heart hammered. Her father was dead.

Door opened.

"Robert-Lee Watkins, this your baby. I been both mother and father for nine years."

He wasn't surprised. "Come in." His voice higher than her father's voice. Short brown-skinned man in brown pants. Slippers.

"You haven't spent one red cent on this child. Haven't put a pair of britches on this baby. I'm going to make a concert artist out of this baby . . ."

Quiet.

He stepped back.

Angela pushed her in.

The door closed. She didn't know her mother would be back. Her father was dead. Her mother gone.

The rug was quiet to her feet. Thin white curtains draped two tall windows. She sat. Rubbed her hand into soft cushion. Her father. Dead. Her blue glass reflection in the coffee table. Couldn't see the bright pain in her eyes. Soft knot burning in her throat. Her father was dead. She might die.

Upstairs somebody made a ruckus. Children rumbled. Laughed. Abeba's face, solemn. Heard every sound.

The stranger whose voice was higher than her father's and who was not her father came toward her.

"Abeba, this is your Aunt Carolyn."

"Hello."

A special quiet. The lady looked into her eyes.

"Karen? Sheila?"

They ran down the steps.

"This is your cousin, Abeba."

"Oh." They stood with shiny earrings in their ears. Hair pressed. Shiny.

"Say hello."

"Hello." They ran back upstairs.

The room, dark. Remember the brown colors when her father was dying. He drank the water. It was cold. Dark.

"Do you like the Christmas tree?" Aunt Carolyn asked.

"Yes." She hadn't seen the tree. Yes. It was full and fresh.

Christmas. The house so tight with company voices. The gramophone playing. People danced. Stood and smoked. Drank. New cold air cut the room each time the company opened the door. Abeba went upstairs to her room. Sat, squeezed away from the company. She peeked through the door. Watched a man and a woman kiss on the mouth. Watched people pass by.

Someone opened the door wide.

"You not Karen. You too big. What's your name, baby?"

"Abeba Lavoisier."

"You say your name is Baby? You not no baby, sugar. You's a big girl. Come on down with the company. Enjoy yourself. It's Christmas."

Abeba followed in her gray jumper. Middy blouse.

"Where's your mother?"

"She's not here."

"Where's your father?"

"He's dead."

"I'm sorry to hear that."

"My mother said this here present is for you." Karen gave her a gift. Karen's nose wide like her nose. Her skin the same color as Abeba's skin.

"Open it."

"I want to open it after while."

Karen snatched the box. Opened it.

Abeba grabbed it. "You already have too many presents!"

Karen left.

Mr. Branches offered her beer.

"Al!" his wife said. "Don't offer her no beer. She's just a child and her mother don't drink."

"Where's your mother?"

"She went."

Al started singing sideways. He just neverminded her mother.

> *Pull down the shade*
> *Turn off the light*
> *Honey babe don't disappoint me tonight*

Wicked. Mrs. Branches said Al couldn't hold his liquor. His mouth slanted. Eyes closed. Perhaps she could go back upstairs now. To the dark.

"Who this sitting here looking so pretty?"

"Abeba Lavoisier."

"A who?" He acted funny. "I'm Rob-Lee's big brother." He staggered. "Unc-kle. Ralphie."

He almost fell on her.

She stared into the wide face. Rough. Marked.

"Look just like Rob-Lee." He picked loosely at his pockets. "If I had a knowed my brother's baby be here . . ." He searched for something. Looked at her, eyes half-closed. Chucked her under the chin. "If I had a knowed my brother's baby be here, I'd a brung you a little something for Christmas."

He was drunk.

"Santa Claus brung you a doll?"

"Yes."

He pulled at the woolen hair. "That's nice."

"Ralphie!"

"Well. If it ain't my brother C-J." He said, "This your youngest uncle."

"How you mean?" C-J looked around when he talked. His hands wiggled in his pockets.

"Stupid!" Uncle Ralphie took a deep breath. "Can't you see she look just like your brother, hummmmmmmm?"

He told a lady. "This here's my niece. I'm going to give her this half-dollar . . . for a present. Christmas present."

"No thank you."

"You can take it, honey. Ralphie's your uncle."

"Thank you."

"Give your uncle a kiss."

His purply lip drooped in the way of his face.

"Go on."

She kissed him quickly on his scratchy chin. Smelled rotten grapes in his mouth.

"Tender thing." He kissed her. Told the lady. "She plays the Halle—halle—lujah Chorus."

"No."

"Yes she do. Go on round to the piano and play . . . Hey cut that thing off. Baby here's fixing to play the Hallelu—jah Chorus." Moved through the criss-crossing voices to the music. Waved his arms. Stopped the machine. "There."

In the sudden silence, voices dropped.

"Ralph, put the music on."

"Baby's fixing to play the Ha—hallelujah. Chorus. Play."

The company came closer. Chewed and looked at her.

She breathed. Wheezing.

"Does she play?"

"How old is she?"

They ate. Grease on their mouths.

"Go on, Abeba," Aunt Carolyn said.

"I—I. I! Don't ha—ha—ha. Ve. The—music."

Aunt Carolyn put the record on.

> *I asked you for a kiss*
> *You gave me a smack*
> *Honey babe you got to learn*
> *To kiss back*

This might be hell. The smoke and bright light. Evil music.

Uncle Ralphie left her. Soon came back carrying a plate. Gave her a napkin. Set them on her lap. Fork. He smiled.

Christmas.

6   After eleven days at camp, Abeba woke to find blood on
her clothes. The sheets. She worked stealthily in the bathroom, rinsing her underpants. Wiping her legs. Tears filled her
eyes. It didn't hurt. But she must have cut herself. In such a personal place . . . Back to Brooklyn. Narrow streets. Moist airless
streets. Evening fights. Shouts. Voices rising. Sharpened quiet.
Somebody killed. All because she had been so careless. She wiped
away fresh blood.

The door opened.

"Hi, Abeba."

"Oh. Elvira."

Elvira had cried the first night. Why would she cry? Want to go
back home? Abeba had come down to the bottom bunk. Put her
arms around Elvira, until she went to sleep. In the big room with
forty Italian girls who sang radio songs. Songs she didn't know. In
the nights large and dark she remembered Jackson. Mamma Habblesham. Rooster. This was the Saratoga Camp for Young Girls.
Why would anyone want to go home the first night?

Abeba pretended to be washing her hands and face. Now she
would have to go home.

"See you later," Elvira said.

"Okay."

Abeba was alone. It was the end of tall trees. Cold mornings.
Evening fires. The end of Saratoga horses who exercised nodding

their heads. Walking. Their sides breathing. No more long tables outside filled with sandwiches. No more hikes. She knew. It was too good to last.

The camp girls jumped into the icy lake. Shocked. Chattering. Elvira threw off her robe, ran with her towel, searching for Abeba's brown, naked body.

"Where's Abeba?"

Abeba stood in the big kitchen filled with metal ware. Three stainless steel sinks. Four industrial refrigerators. Freezers. High tables. Angela worked four burners turning out hotcakes for breakfast.

"I hurt myself," Abeba said.

Her mother turned cakes. As though she didn't hear. Finally put out the fire. Left the kitchen. She'd so often said, Abeba was full of pain as an old woman. Told the doctor. Doctor put her on special diet. No pork. No beef. No fried foods. Just a little stewed chicken. Lamb. Doctor said get your daughter away from Stone Avenue. Or you won't have a daughter. Asthma. She'll die before you die. Die! Angela's own mother died. And she grieved. She said doctor, I'm both mother and father to this child. Can't give Abeba country trips. Very next day, lady she worked for said Angela, come go with me to summer camp. It was just the thing. Mountains. Sunshine. Water from fresh springs. Abeba was a new person.

Lord, help her with this child. Now it was something else.

Angela walked to the dormitory.

Abeba followed.

Lay on her back. Angela spread her daughter's legs. Looked. Said nothing. Went out and came back with a clean cloth. Folded it. Pinned it to Abeba's panties.

"No lake for you today." Her voice was soft. "You're a woman now."

Down at the lake the girls yelled her name. "Abeba!" Pushed and splashed each other. "Come in."

"I can't go in." She sat with her legs close together.

"How come?"

"Yeah. How come?" Water dripped from their faces.

They came toward her splashing water. Laughing.

"Girls!" Miss Hayes called. "Girls!"

When the counselor turned her back, Joan splashed from the water. Her long legs wet and shining.

"How old are you?" Joan asked.

"Eleven and three-quarters."

"I was eleven when I started. It doesn't hurt."

"I know."

"You bleed for a week then it goes away."

"It goes away?"

"Did you think you bleed to death?"

Girl-voices shot high into summer sun. So close, yet drifting to the far side of thought. It seemed that somewhere the whole soft earth was vibrant and bleeding. Sun soaked her shining body. Soft-black mystery. To bleed and not die. The deep green trees filled the Saratoga mountain. Light bounced from the mountains. The air stretched warm and touched the bright blue water. A woman. She was a woman now.

"Abeba, suppose you tell us a story," Miss Hayes said.

Forty-one faces circled the night fire.

"Well . . ." Abeba thought. "There was a lady who lived down South."

"Where?" Anna asked.

"North Carolina."

"Oh."

"She had a little daughter."

"What was her name?"

"Alice." Her hand pulled up crabgrass. "Sometimes they used to have boiled peanuts for supper."

The girls laughed. "Boiled peanuts."

"I wouldn't eat them," Anna said.

"Miss Hayes, is there such a thing as boiled peanuts?"

"Maria, will you shut up and let Abeba tell the story? Miss Hayes, make Maria shut up."

"I just want to know."

"So what happened?"

"Well, one day the lady got sick."

"Did she die?"

"Will you shut up and stop asking questions? Miss Hayes!"

Abeba spoke to the fire. "She didn't die right away. But later on."

"This story is too sad."

"It's a good story."

"So what did the little girl Alice do?"

Abeba heard through warm fire. Her body opened, quietly bleeding. "Naturally she cried."

"So who took care of the little girl?"

"Her father," Maria said.

"Be quiet!" Anna said.

"She's right," Abeba said. "Her father took care of her."

"Is that the end?"

Summer coming to an end and camp almost over. Forty Italian girls for the first two weeks. Next Jewish girls, two weeks. Last Polish girls two weeks. Angela had cooked for all those girls. Abeba played.

Special events day came. Eleven- and twelve-year-olds lined up for foot races. Abeba with them.

"Girls I'm not going to yell," Miss Hayes had been yelling all morning. All summer. "All girls for the potato race. If you can't be cooperative, we'll call it off!"

That got them.

Miss Hayes' arm in the air. Whistle.

Off they flew. Abeba not thinking about winning. Just moving in a hurry. Running. Bend and snatch this wooden potato.

Angela watched. Laughed.

Soon Abeba tumbled over the starting line, the others close to her heels.

Angela grunted.

They went over to the water. Miss Hayes hollered them quiet and soon the water was full of little arms working. Breast stroke. Backstroke. Face float. Butterfly. Dog paddle.

Abeba went in with the backstrokers. Her arms cut the water straight as arrows. When she came from the water, she shook her head. Waited for the other swimmers. Then it came to her. She was first. Miss Hayes shouting, "First place, Abeba Lavoisier!" Came over. Pulled her wet arm into the air. Pinned a ribbon to her wet chest.

When Abeba rode back to Brooklyn with her mother, the edges of her hair were coppery red. Saratoga sun. The ride home, so smooth. She was a woman now. With the mountain and tall tree. With the summer night. A woman.

7　　　After four autumns, Abeba fifteen, tall as Angela stood
　　　before the mirror. Opened a small jar of vanishing cream.
Tapped a white spot on her nose, forehead, both cheeks, chin.
Rubbed it in. Combed her hair. She was a sophomore at Girls
High. White school in a white neighborhood. Her clothes too
small. Blouse tight across her bosoms. Skirt tight across her hips.

Angela watched. Pretended to write the shopping list. "Where's
your ribbons?" she said.

"But I'm in high school."

Angela grabbed Abeba's head. Pulled it down. Braided three
tight braids. Threaded ribbons through her hair.

"There's one woman in this house. Pull those ribbons out if you
want to."

Abeba, stunned, straightened. She'd only said I'm in high
school. It was Angela said you're a woman. When she was eleven.
Bleeding. Abeba glanced at her reflection. Large white ribbons.

Outside, two doors down, Clyde and Leroy sat with Big John,
Ohio. Sat on the stoop before the store-front church.

"You young men disgrace God and sit right before His church
drinking that bad liquor."

"Good morning, Sister Angel and your beautiful daughter."

"Don't throw away your lives on the bottle."

Abeba stood by. Held the shopping bag.

"Bottle'll leave you broke."

"Sure will."

"Make you fall down. Bust your head wide open."

They laughed. Cut it short.

Abeba looked past them. Never asked for anything. Money. For clothes. Movies. Parties. Nothing. Just to take out the ribbons. She stood straight in the over-worn clothes. Thoughts tangled. Her teachers mailed postcards from Europe. Praised her work. Her parents. Why? Why was Angela so angry?

"Liquor eat your liver out."

"Yes it will."

"Rob you of your young life."

"Yes it will."

"Come on down to the church."

"Be there Sunday next." They all talking at once.

"Don't fool me now."

"I be there."

"We be there."

"Throw that bottle out."

"This my last bottle."

"Let's go, Abeba."

They watched her. Dress wrinkled across solid hips. Angela five feet three inches. Close to one hundred and seventy pounds. Abeba slim, walked with her mother.

"Why is it that woman always catch *me* with the bottle?" Ohio asked.

"You the one got the bottle."

"And think she got a baby girl for a daughter. Hair all tied up in bows."

"Piano Girl's a grown woman, man."

"A real lady."

"Wouldn't mind having me a old lady like that one day. She play the piano and I just lay back listening. If she got something to say to me, voice pretty and polite."

"Most the women on Stone Avenue'll cuss you before they speak."

"They not making too many like her."

"Instead of trying to see who she got for a daughter, that woman's out here worrying about *my* liquor. By now she should have figgered out why her daughter gets sick every winter, and the ambulance got to come take her on out to Kings County. Got her own daughter out in the dark. Five or six years ago I hear somebody real quiet tapping on my door. Opened it and there was Piano Girl talking about sweet potato pies, thirty-five cents each. Probably been into places where somebody just OD'd. Police just carry the body out and she talking about sweet potato pies!"

"Don't make no sense."

"Day after that I find out her father dead. And she out here trying to help her mother make ends meet since she ain't got no people."

"Piano Girl!"

"Hello, Ohio."

"What's happening. How you feel today?"

"All right."

"We looking for you to make it big. Somebody from Stone Avenue got to make it."

Abeba smiled.

"You don't be out in the streets too much after dark like you use to."

"My uncle comes now and sells the pies for me."

"Your uncle?"

"Yes."

"Didn't know you had a uncle. That's real nice. Now you got more time to put on your studies."

"Yes."

"Don't have to be looking out for a bunch of niggers and drunks sneaking up behind you and snatching up all your pies."

Abeba laughed.

"You sure got a pretty voice. I'm a let you go now and get into them books, so you have all the answers in class tomorrow."

"Good-bye."

"That must be him," Ohio told Clyde, Leroy. Big John.

"Who?"

"The uncle."

They examined a man who came from Abeba's building carrying a bag.

"Didn't know piano girl had no people."

"Say, brother!" Ohio called the man.

"What's happening, man?"

"You got any pies for me?"

"You got thirty-five cents?"

Ohio tried to get credit. "Well, dig. Give me the pie today and I'll pay you tomorrow."

"You might be dead tomorrow, brother. I can't take chances with my niece's pies."

"You Piano Girl's people?"

"Name's C-J."

Ohio extended his hand. "Ohio. This LeRoy. Big John, Clyde. Your niece's a genius, man."

C-J's face broke into smiles. "She's a real lady. Ain't but fifteen years old. Talk like a telephone operator. Voice so soft. And smart as a whip. She be talking about this thing and that and I'm saying um-humm, um-humm, but to tell you the truth, she lost me long ago, Jim. But I try to sit there drinking these little cups of cocoa and not say too much . . ."

The four watched him carefully.

"I better get on out of here. I sell most these pies to the men down to the factory. Got a wife and two little ones of my own, so I got to head home." He shook hands again. "Nice talking to you, brothers." Looked at Ohio's very lean body. "Save up thirty-five cents, brother. Get one of these pies. Put some fat on your ribs."

The four watched C-J walk down the street. A shambles of a man. Autumn coat too large. Wide leg of his pants flapping as he walked a tight walk.

"That man ain't nothing like his niece."

"He got troubles."

"We all got troubles."

"See how he come over so quick when you call him and start running off at the mouth like he couldn't stop?"

"But I give him credit for looking out for his niece. Like he said, he got his own family, but still he keeping his niece off the streets . . . Listen at Piano Girl."

Upstairs, two doors over, Abeba's glissandos and arpeggios broke into Mendelssohn's moody "Spinning Song."

Ohio smiled quietly. Spoke to himself. "C-J . . . Piano Girl's uncle!"

Late January, Abeba heard C-J's voice in the bottom hall. Waited upstairs at the opened door.

"How's school, Little One?" He roughed her hair.

"All right."

He smiled at the two cups set out on the table.

"Still making A's?"

"Yes." Abeba wanted to talk. About school. Trigonometry. To

laugh about the "donkey method." Proving triangles congruent by angle, side, side. But C-J was slow at figures. He said three fours. Two fours make eight and four more give you twelve. He wrote in careful, rounded script. He said you write fast. Ever think about being a secretary? She said a concert artist. He said oh. Pardon me.

They sat. Drank cocoa. She watched his face. Eyes far apart. Thick eyebrows. The black dots on his skin filled with hair.

Behind him, afternoon light caught a few places on the hard wall. Naked, except for a five and dime picture of Jesus praying. Faded halo around his head. Outside the room, the building ajumble with new noises. Tumblings in tiny rooms filtered past her consciousness. Brighter noise heard in layers grafted to the back of her thoughts of three months ago when she met C-J in the street.

A door slammed. Startled her.

"Let me get these pies sold," Uncle C-J said. His lips were big and soft. He lifted the little cup. Drank the last. "You make such nice little cups of cocoa."

"Would you like some more?"

He swallowed the second cup. Stray drops of warm cocoa spilled over his lips. He looked at her quickly. Wiped his mouth with his hands. "Sorry about that."

He had tiny red veins in his eyes. His eyelashes curled tight. Sometimes he leaned against the piano bench, his stomach strained against the belt. His underarms smelled sweaty. He chewed small things on the tip of his tongue. Instead of putting it on a tissue, he thooped it out. Half-humming. Sour notes. Last Christmas he brought her a green skirt. Everyday he came and drank two cups of cocoa.

"So what you want for Easter, Little One?"

"Easter!"

"You want a Easter bonnet?" He tugged her braid. "Ain't this something. In high school, wearing pigtails. But you cute just the same. Don't know how someone ugly like my brother have a baby so cute." He put his arms around her. "Thanks for the cocoa."

Monday, after school, Abeba walked down Stone Avenue with Peter Castle. A white boy who carried her books.

Ohio and them studied this boy. Studied Piano Girl.

"How you doing, Piano Girl?"

"All right."

"How's school?"

"All right."

Studied her skirt flapping at the back of her legs. Here she was walking with a white boy. Blond and blue eyes too. Stopped at her building. Gave Abeba her books. Walked off. That something!

"Come to Stone Avenue!"

"That something!"

Girls High and Boys High had given a joint assembly. They knew each other from grammar school. For the finale played a duet that left the audience screaming. The girls jealous of her. She didn't expect Peter to walk her home. Carry her books. But they kept talking. About concerts. Pianos. Teachers. Music. Chopin. How many hours it took her to learn a nocturne. Same for him. It would be fun, next year. To do it again. They walked through cold without feeling cold. And suddenly she was home.

April second, Abeba heard C-J's voice. Opened the door while he climbed the stairs. Her old blouse tucked neatly into her green skirt. Cups of cocoa set on the table.

"Hello, Little One." He carried a present. Kissed her. His face, freshly shaved, smelled of red Lifebuoy.

"I see you fixed me some cocoa."

"Yes."

His shirt was clean, fine-striped. He was going someplace.

"How's school?"

"All right."

He drank two cups of cocoa. Fast. "I got your present."

"Already!"

"But something I been meaning to mention. Didn't figure you to have no white boyfriend."

"Boyfriend!"

"In fact, I didn't expect you to have a boyfriend period."

Abeba shot up from the table.

"I don't have a boyfriend."

"I seen you walking with a white boy."

"Peter Castle?"

"That his name?"

"He just plays duets!"

"You all sit to the piano? He rub his white butt up against your butt?"

"What?"

"I can't say he came in here."

"You're not my father!"

"I love you better than your father. I know I'm not your father."

"Keep your present. You have no right to spy on me."

"No . . ."

"I'll give you back your skirt. I can sell my own pies."

He came to her. She cried quietly into his clean shirt.

He kissed her. On the forehead. Lifted her chin. Kissed her lips.

Abeba's eyes sprang open.

"I wouldn't hurt you," he said. Voice unclean with softness. His hands hard on her body. "I won't hurt you, baby."

She pulled back. Puzzled.

"Your Uncle C-J's going to make a woman out of you." His hands gathered up her skirt.

She plunged it down.

"I won't hurt you baby."

He pulled her head up. Kissed her mouth. Pushed his sloppy lips against her clenched teeth.

Abeba's head swung crazy circles. She punched him. Stunned. He slapped her. Slapped her. His breath smelled of cocoa.

"I don't want to hurt you baby."

"Please, Uncle C-J."

He shook back and unzipped his pants.

Abeba was in the closet, naked from the waist down. Her face puffed from screaming. Crying. It seemed she had burst every vein in her neck. She came out. The green skirt lay on the floor. Pink snuggies. Her father was dead. Dead! Why did he have to be dead! Abeba's head throbbed and ached. Lightly bruised tissues throbbed and ached. She thought she was pregnant. She burned in hell.

Saturday afternoon, Abeba found her mother in the narrow hall kitchen.

"Mommie."

Her mother threw salt. Turned meat. Salted. "Speak up, Abeba. You talk like a little mouse. You're in high school now." She salted meat. Turned. Salted.

"Uncle C-J came last night."

"Did he get the pies?"

"Yes, Mommie . . . I told him you weren't home. He. He—he tried to—take—off—my clothes."

Angela put the pan in the oven. "Your Uncle C-J's a dirty rascal. Ugly Watkins brothers. God don't like ugly."

Abeba waited.

"Empty the ice-pan please ma'am."

She pulled out the round basin, emptied the water into the sink.

"Go finish your lessons. Then come peel potatoes."

Monday came. Uncle C-J. Abeba didn't understand he was wearing protection. Expected to grow a round belly. Woke suddenly in the night. Dreamed. Something touched her while she slept. Vanished when she woke.

"Piano Girl! What's got you out here looking so sad? What happened to your smile?"

"Hello, Ohio."

"I realize you got your uncle to look out for you, but you got me too."

Abeba looked into Ohio's lean face.

"Thank you." She spoke so soberly that Ohio stood staring long after she went into the building.

In summer, she counseled camp. Autumn returned. C-J returned. God kept giving her one more chance. Every month, blood flowed.

Winter, again. Uncle C-J. She lost school days. Her asthma grew worse.

March the twenty-first, Uncle C-J knocked.

Abeba played the piano. Louder. Louder.

Irene called, "Abeba!" Said, "Sometimes she get to playing the piano, she can't hear less you holler. Abeba! Your uncle here to visit with you."

Music stopped.

Abeba opened the door.

"How are you, Little One?"

"Have a nice visit," Irene said. Carried her fourth baby on her hip.

C-J closed the door. Smiled. His eyes far apart. He dropped his pants. Sat to loose his laces. Bent forward. Abeba quiet. Reached for the metronome. Cracked sharp corner against his head.

He stayed bent. A long moment. Seemed he would crash to the floor.

Abeba watched. Her face filled with sweat. Blood spurted from his head. Pain shot through her body. Now! He was a woman now. Sweat rolled down her face. Salt water spread under her tongue.

"Girl!" He snatched the metronome. "You could kill somebody." He pulled up his pants. Wiped his head. Lifted his red hand to slap her. Stopped. Cursed quietly. Left.

For the first time in a year, Abeba went out to sell Angela's pies.

8   Abeba, eighteen years old, turned in her bed. The green army blanket scratched her chin. Her mother's warm body smells filled her nose. Her mother soft snoring slept like a quiet mountain. Just above her head the light of a new winter morning. The piano, oiled and black, collected weight and straight lines in the February light. Remember when she stood at the window, when she was six years old? Watched the children go to school. She needed to register. Remember Oliver? The boy who pushed her down. In the quiet she thought of September. The white sheet. Police. The water was cold at the lake. The water was cold in her father's glass.

Her mother turned. "You wake, Abeba?"

"Good morning, Mommie."

"It's graduation day. Graduation day." Angela cleared phlegm. Adjusted her head on the warm pillow. Spoke with eyes closed. "Graduation day."

Downstairs the morning wind toyed with trash. Iron gate rattled in the storekeeper's window. Jesus stared in young watercolor, stared from the silent door of the sanctified church. Thin leafless trees shook and were still. Pigeons walked and pecked the winter ground. Sparrows hopped about. Dogs urinated and slept in hallways. It was a sacred day. Winter on Stone Avenue. February fourth, graduation day.

Abeba's body was fragile. Stiff with joy as she bathed. She

soaped her breasts in a tub of warm water heated pot by pot in the hall kitchen. Washed her underarms until the hairs whistled. Her shoulder and arm muscles strong from years of music. Soaped firm buttocks. Legs. Ankles, feet.

Before the room heater, Abeba oiled her body. Dressed. Pulled on cotton-soft underwear. Lace-trimmed slip. Nylon stockings. Gifts. Black patent leather shoes. Pulled the white dress over her head. Her mother's hand gently tugged it in place. It fell smooth, touched her feet. With the towel over her shoulders, she loosed her hair. Pulled out strips of brown paper. Hairpins. Poured heated olive oil into her palms. Rubbed her scalp. Her face in the mirror wondered at itself. Bright glow in her eyes. Her skin. Hair parted, combed and brushed, she pulled off the towel. Brown-toned white neckline, brilliant against her brown skin. Puffed sleeves full of shadows and soft cloth.

She put on the school ring. Reached for the winter coat, wine colored with velveteen collar and cuffs. Special gift from the pastor and his wife. Corsage of pink roses. Gift from her mother.

"First knock on Irene's door. Let her see your pretty dress."

Irene hollered. "Please look at Abeba!"

Doors opened. Downstairs neighbors. Across the street neighbors.

"Lord have mercy," Grandma Iris said. "Look at this child."

"Turn around."

"You too beautiful."

"Well, Piano Girl. You get that sheepskin today."

"She's a natural genius man."

"Wish I had a stayed in school."

"I don't know you," Grandma Iris kept saying. "Just don't know you."

At Girls High there was magic female feeling in the heavy stone building. Iron fence and winter lawn. The flutter of girl-women voices. Flutter of white dresses snatched and puffed in frosty wind.

"Mrs. Lavoisier?"

"Yes?"

"You've done a wonderful job with Abeba."

The French teacher hugged Abeba. Her arms trembling.

"Thank you, ma'am." Angela was polite. Spoke in her graduation voice.

"I wish I spoke French as well as Abeba."

"That so!" Angela laughed.

She squeezed Abeba's arm. "You look like a model!" Pressed a card into her hand. Hurried off hailing students. Teachers.

"Abeba!"

"Mommie! It's Mary Ann Joniek!" Abeba ran in stiff new shoes. Threw her arms around her friend. Heard Mary Ann's father and mother talking to her mother.

"Abeba! Is that you?"

She turned. "Annette!" Hugged. "Florence, Gloria, Colleen. My goodness. Barbara. Oh, no." They laughed and cried in a big circle.

The auditorium, first filled with rushing ushers. Aisles moved with talking parents. Faculty. The deep-ceilinged auditorium weighted with drapery. Grand piano to the right. The auditorium stood still, sacred now as chords struck brought graduates in a billow of silent white. Angela straining to see the dark face among the graduates.

Abeba came through the door afloat in the new hour. She knew. Now, as the chords opened in ancient white-flower, she was a woman. Her dress falling about her. Soft rustling of slips. She couldn't quite touch the tall velvet silence that settled when the graduates sat. Stood again to sing. When Alberta Lorenz, a tall red-head, gave the salutation.

The principal praised parents. Students. Put on her glasses and handed out awards. Applause broke like summer sunrise.

"Abeba Lavoisier, for Cooperation in Government." She applauded. Abruptly stood, walked past Mary Ann who grabbed her hand. The new shoes stiff to the sloping floor. As rehearsed, she reached for the award with her left, shook with her right. The wide audience below watched. Clapped again.

"Abeba Lavoisier for Class Musician."

The noise stunned her. Rapid clapping of hands. Shouts. Disoriented, she found her way. Noise quieted. She reached with her left, the principal held her right.

"For the parents who have never heard this remarkable student play, you're in for a great treat today." To Abeba, "May you have a successful career as a musician. Girls High has been honored to have you."

At the piano, Abeba breathed deeply. Smiled at Mrs. Brodsky, music teacher, who sat ready to turn seventeen pages. Abeba opened the book. Page one, Mozart's Sonata in A. Familiar patterns. Bright black notes, flags, lines, bars, spaces, rests. Ready. In the heart of the graduation hour, the dry heat that stuck her lips to teeth, vanished. Her hands struck the even majestic opening. Gathered breath from the years. Music, like soft fire, filled the ceiling. Dropped to the intimate mood of daily life. The ocean gray of winter dawn. Fragile tones of sunset-red. Her hands remembered winter days, days like letters written in pencil. When she looked from high windows. When she heard a sharpening quiet. Head snapped with crushing crescendos. Her hands bent colors into rapid wheels turning. She watched patterns of pages, dots, trills that brought sudden bright tulips of young children. She nodded. Mrs. Brodsky turned pages. Again and again until finally a brief crescendo. Then quiet-quiet notes teasing a musical idea, quiet of new thoughts forming. A struggle to touch the escaping dream, the presence of a new day. The world an uncertain planet waiting outside the tall windows. The whole room still when the music ended.

Half-surprised, Abeba stood to find the audience standing. She bowed. Wondered. They kept clapping.

Mrs. Brodsky wiped her eyes. Leaned into the microphone. "The parents of Abeba Lavoisier should be indeed proud today. Your daughter is a first-class musician."

In the applause that rose and continued, there was the voice of an old midwife. Saying, "Hush your mouth."

9 How many years had she slept with her mother. Cramped. Asthmatic. Her mother now slept in the bedroom. Abeba alone in the living room of their new apartment. She had paid for it. Went to work, as though in a dream. Took loud subways rushing into Manhattan. Rode crowded elevators to the twenty-second floor where it seemed she attended a taller school. A freshman, without homework. Evenings she cooked in their private kitchen, bristling white. Pots washed and scrubbed shiny after each use. Taught music to little children. Read African history at the Brooklyn library.

Slowly she began to understand. This was not school. Slowly, then suddenly, the money, like magic, had turned into this pretty place. Soft-smooth walls. Maroon-gray floor. Glass cover on the ceiling light. Her graduation picture on the wall.

The spring brought wedding invitations. Sometimes to attend. Sometimes to play. Nobody asked Abeba to marry until one man stopped her in the street.

"I got me a good job," he said.

Was he talking to her?

"Working for the railroad."

Abeba's eyes narrowed. She started to move on.

"Wait a minute . . . I'm asking you to marry me."

Her mouth opened. She rushed off. Heard him calling to her. He was crazy.

But it made the spring complete. Filled with lacy-cool days. Dreams.

Summer after graduation was sudden. August weeks blistered. Windows on Glendale filled with spinning fans. Tempers flying. Folk put out a line of wash and pulled it in the same hour. Stiff dry. Jerome the ice boy came three times last week, carrying ice wrapped in filthy burlap. Neighbors began to answer each other. Abeba heard them through the night. Again this Saturday night. Loud music pounded the streets. Singing. Hey-bop-a-ree-bop! Hollering. Laughing. Feet noisy on wooden stairs. The noise lifted through night darkness. Finally close to morning, quiet.

Abeba had a brief sleep.

Most folk were still in bed by day. They rose at noon. Ate cold melon. Too hot for church this Sunday.

Abeba played for a handful of sweating Christians at First Baptist. Late Sunday afternoon, music fell in heavy drifts. The scattering of people fanned. Wiped sweat. Abeba's eyes sticky with heat, glanced vaguely past hymn chords. She wished she could stretch out. Sleep. Voices lagged through the last verse. "Day Is Dying in the West." Then a new voice, bright as wine, lifted through the heat.

Abeba turned.

A small man, someone new to First Baptist. Mouth thrown open wide.

They sat.

"Young man," Reverend Judges called, "come forward and speak a word for the Lord."

He came to the front. Walked swiftly, one arm swinging. Turned to face the empty summer church.

"Pastor, associates, sisters and brothers. I'm Reverend Brother

Daniel A. Torch bringing you greetings from First Church, St. Augustine, Florida."

"Amen."

"I'm no stranger in the house of the Lord."

"Amen."

"Come to New York five years ago with three brothers. Another one already here. Don't like to see Sunday pass less I worship in the house of the Lord."

"Amen."

"We had old-fashioned parents who gave us that old-time religion."

"That's all right." Feet patted. Heads shook. "It's all right."

"I'm no stranger to God."

"Well."

"God called me to preach when I was fourteen. And I didn't want to be no preacher."

"Have mercy."

"You know how we black people are. We want to be doctors and lawyers, but please don't call me to be no preacher. But God called me when I was fourteen years old."

"Mercy Jesus."

"I didn't want to answer when He called me."

"Better answer when He calls." Fans flurried. Heads shook. "Got to answer when He calls."

"Took me ten years to say 'Here am I, O Lord. Send me'!"

"It's all right."

"Testify, young man."

His voice dropped. "I'd like to give my testimony in song, this afternoon. If the organist will accompany me."

"Anything you can sing, Sister Abeba can play. Play like lightning and thunder."

First Church laughed.

Abeba examined the visitor. His face sweating. Eyed his dark blue jacket. Blue pants. Different shades. Soft white collar home pressed. If the piano hadn't blocked her, she would have seen the worn shoes. Shaped to his feet.

"We use to have a quartet," he said. "Four brothers. But God called our oldest brother home. Joshua. That was his name. Hasn't even been a year."

The church listened.

"He was my closest brother and I didn't see how I could go on living. He had done so much for the rest of us." His voice cracked. He bounced forward a little. Waved his arm as he spoke. "All I could think was I might as well die too."

"God can make a way out of no way."

"My Lord."

"So I'm going to sing one of his favorites. 'Couldn't Hear Nobody Pray'!"

"Amen."

He stood still a moment. Head pulled back, eyes closed. Began in a small controlled voice:

> Oh Lord, I couldn't hear nobody pray
> Couldn't hear nobody pray.
> Way down yonder by myself
> And I couldn't hear nobody pray.

The South's heat soft in the body of his song. Sweat rolled down his face. Tears. Soft collar crumpled under the oily water on his neck.

> Seeking Jesus
> Couldn't hear nobody pray

> Chilly Jordan
> Couldn't hear nobody pray
> Crossing over
> Couldn't hear nobody pray
> Into Caanan
> Couldn't hear nobody pray.
> Oh Lord . . .

His voice wide as the sun, filled with pain. Crying for his dead brother. He paused. And the church sucked breath as he pulled his head forward, opened his mouth to one side and the blackest pure bass, like a thick tree, broke bedrock of pain. Voice dropped lower and lower until the whole church slipped into the low-dark voice and cried out.

> Troubles over
> Couldn't hear nobody pray
> Troubles over
> Couldn't hear nobody pray
> Troubles over . . .

He began to snatch his head. Repeating. As though his dead brother touched him and he would sing forever. Voice dropping softer. "Troubles over," dropping until it turned to silence in the heat.

In an eternal moment, Daniel Torch opened his eyes. Bowed. Took his seat. Left others on their feet, arms stretched to Jesus. Calling Him. Calling Him.

Abeba dried her sweating hands on her skirt. Wiped tears from her eyes.

Reverend Judges laughed the holy laugh.

The church laughed with him.

The bare wooden floor of the church dining room echoed foot-steps of women who carried platters of cake from the kitchen. Echoed conversations about the young man. Talented with such a deep voice. August light fell through tall windows. Fell across the four tables, covered with white paper cloths. Folded napkins. Paper cups. Butter sponge cake, chocolate cake. Tiny baskets of peanuts and mints.

"This collation fit for a king," Daniel said.

The members laughed.

He held Abeba's chair. Sat across from her.

"Voice so deep. Remind me of Roland Hayes."

"Paul Robeson."

"And such a little man."

"Little fellow, big voice," Angela said. Laughed with her mouth wide open. Laughed at her own joke.

"Just keep singing for the Lord."

"Yes ma'am."

Mother Agnes laid a hand on Daniel's shoulder. "Young man, just keep singing for the Lord."

"Yes ma'am."

"Never mind what's happening in the world."

"Yes ma'am."

"Nothing out there for you." Her voice was aged, but she spoke so strong.

Daniel stood, now. Polite. Listening. Without his jacket, he looked smaller. Slim shoulders. Small waist. Belt pulled through his pants and fed through several loops.

"I know what I'm talking about. I'm from St. Augustine too!"

"Oh, shur!" Daniel kissed her. "Come all the way to New York and find someone from my home town."

"You liable to find some of everything in New York." She walked off. Leaning on other shoulders. Talking. Talking.

Abeba struggled to bring things into focus. The song. His standing there. Speaking so close to her.

"You speak so nice and clipped, I took you for a native New Yorker." He broke pieces of cake. Chewed. "This is good cake." Pressed his fingers into the crumbs and flicked them into his mouth. Eyes thinking other thoughts. "You had me fooled."

"I did?"

"Thought you were in your twenties or thirties. That was before I got a good look at you."

"Oh."

"You play real professional."

"Thank you." Abeba ate a small piece of cake.

"You have sisters?"

"No."

"Brothers?"

"No."

His thick eyebrows sprang up. "That's a surprise. Seemed you would have a sister." He poured more lemon drink. "I got two more brothers in New York. Two sisters back home. One more brother's home."

"All those sisters and brothers!"

"Not counting the ones that died." He squeezed the paper cup. Chewed ice. "Would be nice if you could visit St. Augustine sometime. But you got to be ready for the heat. This little Brooklyn weather just practicing to get hot. St. Augustine can really put out some heat. This heat you got in New York? We take for a cool spell. Hot Florida weather good for orange groves. Palm trees. Persimmon trees. It's beautiful there, I tell you. Of course they give black folks the swamp land. Some old land they don't know what to do with. Guess they feel black folks and alligators can keep an eye on each other."

Abeba laughed. Too loud.

Church folk turned to look.

Daniel lifted the empty cup absentmindedly. Drank air. "St. Augustine such a pretty place, I wouldn't mind staying there if I could make a living. But it's hard to keep living, let alone make a living."

His voice, smooth purple, seemed to come from inside her heart. She breathed cautiously. He spoke. Her head afloat, somewhere in a Florida place. Where garden snakes came into the house. The house raised from the ground because the full moon carried water into the yards.

Daniel Torch stared back into a moment. His small eyes distant. Deep curve in his forehead filled with Florida thoughts. His plump lips Indian black. Smooth.

Abeba drank iced water.

"Spent one year in college, you know. If you live in St. Augustine, got to go three miles to school. Go walking. Had a school house in town for white folks. Ever notice most white folks got wide fleshy legs? Black folks' legs tight?" He smiled at his joke. "But know what?"

"What."

"Didn't mind walking. How much I thought of school. When Papa took me out the eighth grade? That thing hurt me so. Went to the turpentine woods. Dipping gum and just as I was at the front of the class. Everytime I got to thinking about all the dumbbells passing me while I was in the woods . . ." His voice shifted. "If you don't cut that tree just right, gum won't flow." His heavy hand slashed the air. He looked Abeba full in the face.

Startled her.

"Abeba?"

She jumped. "Yes Mommie."

"Let's go home. Got to get out of these sweaty clothes."

"Brother Daniel Torch . . ."

"Abeba!"

"I'm coming . . . We need more men in the choir."

"I'll be here Sunday next, Sister Abeba. I got two brothers in New York with good singing voices. I'll bring them with me."

Abeba breathed the summer street. Warm noisy air.

"Streets full, church empty," Angela said.

The coming cars bright in the evening. Children brushed them, running past.

"Folks like to take vacation from God. So backward." She called to the children. "Walk. Walk. Need to ask your mothers take you to Sunday school. Children half naked in the street. Dirty."

Abeba far away, felt her mother's voice with the annoyance she would feel in a light drizzle. Her skin glowed in the evening light. The way he said goodbye. Called her *Sister* Abeba. She suddenly sensed Angela studying her. "It's cooler now," Abeba said.

Angela grunted. "September come tomorrow. And next year this time, you'll be at Juilliard, God willing."

Abeba's thoughts tight against Daniel's magic singing. She stumbled.

"Watch your step!" Angela's double meanings lost.

Would he bring his brothers?

Thursday evening, there was a new knock.

"Who?"

"Daniel Torch."

"Daniel Torch." Abeba opened the door. Her heart beat with his heart. "Come in."

"Good evening, Sister Abeba."

His hair brushed. Patted close to his head. Face freshly washed. Fresh blue shirt.

He walked past her. "You got to wake me before I take this for a doll house. Pink walls and white curtains. This really is feminine."

"Thank you."

"What a beauty!" He whistled. Stroked the piano.

"Thank you."

"How long you had this piano?"

"Nine years."

"And better than new. Sleek black. Reminds me of a horse we had. Named Jacobs. Course he's dead now. Was most dead when we first got him, but I was just a little boy. Didn't know the difference. Cried just the same." He stroked the piano. "Some beauty."

Then he saw the graduation picture.

Whistled. "Most took this for a wedding photo. Now this is something." He was quiet.

Abeba blushed when he looked at her.

"So when you going to start back to school?"

"Next September."

"Good. Next year I'll have enough saved up pay one year at Columbia. I got the acceptance papers all right, but felt pretty discouraged when I saw the tuition figures. But got to thinking about an African hero. Soldiers came into his home. Butchered up his family. Father, mother, big strapping brothers. Looked at him and laughed. Wouldn't bother to kill him . . ."

"He was crippled," Abeba said.

Daniel looked at her.

"Sundiata!"

He slapped the side of his head. "For crying out loud. Thought I was the only one liked those stories."

"I have an African name."

"That's right . . . You read about the caravan of hundreds of camels carrying gold dust? Traded for salt?"

"Timbuktu. City of close to two hundred schools. Just read about Askia Mohammed Touré."

"Now he was a scholar. Wrong religion! But great scholar, I tell you."

They smiled together.

Daniel looked around. "Mighty quiet in here."

"Mommie's at a club meeting. North Carolina Gleaners."

"No wonder it's so quiet. Your mother has some voice."

"I know."

They stood looking at each other.

"I stopped by, hoped you would go over this solo for me?" He carried his music rolled tight.

"Sure."

She sat.

He stood near. Unbuttoned his shirt cuffs. Folded back neatly to the elbow. Opened top button. His face and neck smooth black against blue shirt.

"I'm a little fellow," he said, "but got a big neck. Make those high notes and button pop straight off." He looked at her. "Whenever you're ready."

She nodded.

He sang.

Many brave souls are asleep in the deep

She felt his eyes on her face. Her neck. Yet when she glanced up, he seemed to be in the faraway place of his music. Until he reached the final moments of his song: "Beware." Her eyes left the page. Caught his eyes, small. Filled with lights. Love. "Beware . . ." His voice tumbled to a final low-low note, "Beware."

"Oh!" Her face was shining.

"Shall we go over that again?"

"It was perfect."

They heard Angela's key turn the lock.

"Good evening, Mommie."

"Good evening, Madame Lavoisier."

"Daniel Torch came by . . ."

"Too late for Daniel Torch."

"Sorry," he said.

"Abeba got to practice her own music. Got no time for you young men . . ."

"Mommie! We were just . . ."

"I . . . ," Daniel said.

"Abeba's got a good education. Part scholarship to Juilliard . . ."

"I'm going."

Angela opened the door.

He left. Hadn't said good-night. Hadn't taken his music.

Angela gave Abeba a special look. Went about settling into the evening.

Lights in Abeba's skin vanished. Troubled look clouded her eyes.

10   Abeba sat at supper, filled with quiet thoughts. Saturday.
          She heard male voices. Female talking outside. Laughing.
This, the third week since Daniel sang at the church. Sang right
here. In the living room.

Angela, quiet, cut her food. Ate. Glanced over at Abeba's full
plate. Served herself apple pie. Ice cream. Swirled the cold sweet
cream over her tongue.

"Daniel Torch is a country boy," Angela said.

Abeba's mind swung around. She saw the hominy, covered
with red sauce and mackerel, cold. Her plate full.

"He's uneducated." Angela rinsed her hands at the faucet.
Wiped wet hands across her mouth. "You got your music lessons
to get out." She sucked loose food from her teeth. "Got to save up
for Juilliard." Paused. Opened the closet, stooped and brought out
a large bag of scraps. Settled at the machine to make aprons. "I
spent too much time working long hours to watch you throw your
life away . . ." The machine stitched. Stopped. Stitched.

"No," Angela said. Bit thread. "No. You can't marry Daniel
Torch!"

"Marry! After you threw him out?"

"Don't you fly up in my face!" The hand wheel turned as Angela's foot worked the pedal. "Lazy, lazy young men. Our men will
never get any place . . ."

"He's saved four hundred dollars!"

"I been both mother and father to you."

"He's going to Columbia."

"He's uneducated. Says 'chutch' instead of 'church.' "

"He's already accepted."

"Then let him go on to college. That will be good for him."

"I thought you'd like a preacher."

"Jack-legged preacher!" The machine picked up Angela's anger. The needle plunged swift stitches into the cloth. "I don't want no young men in this house when I'm not home, you hear me Abeba?" She broke thread. Clipped edges. Lachesis.

"When I was nine, you sent me out in the dark selling pies. You left me alone until midnight." Her muscles locked. "Wh—wh— when! When—I . . ."

Angela stood. Vibrant eyes like bulbs of matches heated, burst into flame. She untied her apron. "Come with me."

It was fully dark when they stepped down three shallow steps. An odd place where a dull window light lit red lettering: Sister Mary, Reader and Spiritual Adviser.

They went through a curtain into a dark room. Oily air shimmered, thick with candle smell. There was a voice. Movement. Abeba's heart pounded, merged with the pulpy blackness. Seemed she might disappear. Her whole body wiped away like excess ink.

"My daughter's man crazy."

Candle lit. Someone grunted. She could see the lady.

"I want to know how many children she going to have."

Doors slammed. Candle flickered tall light and Abeba watched the woman's strange face. Light caught in the creases beneath the eye. Abeba felt a warmth siphoned from her. Her mind atremble spread over her body and spilled its life under the woman's eyes. The woman's hands, hard through Abeba's clothes, rubbed the body. Searched the stomach and pelvis. Stop! Abeba wanted to shout. But heard only a whimper. Hands rubbed her lower back. Felt the soft bosoms. Pulled Abeba close to the fire. She hummed and grunted and felt the forehead. Abeba shook.

"Go outside."

Dazed. By the people laughing. Traffic on 125th Street. Dazed to be in the streets, earth street. To stand. Her hands closed so tight the trimmed nails cut deep prints.

Her mother came out.

"Come on." Her mother's voice distant.

Abeba followed. Had no idea of the reader's words: she would have children. No less than twelve. No more than twenty.

11   Bright sun fell on Daniel's thick hair. On Abeba's face. Splashed the blue velvet.

"What you making?"

"Christmas dress."

He kissed her. In front of his two brothers. Matthew washed the windows that sparkled now. Calvin peeled potatoes.

"So what's going on!" Matthew smiled. He had big eyes. A sporty man. Tall. Six feet. Hair barber cut. Dimples in both cheeks.

"Never mind," Daniel said. "Keep your big eyes on the window." He fingered the pattern. "Mighty thin!" Read French instructions, *"Milieu devant . . . soutenir. Placer sur le droit fil . . ."* Smiled. "A regular lesson."

Kissed her quietly.

They heard Angela move restively in the bedroom. Filled the quiet with conversation.

"Remember how the four of us worked when we first come to New York?"

"Yeah."

"So Joshua come to New York first and find four jobs working at the hospital. But wasn't no kin supposed to work on the same job."

They sat around Abeba.

"So all right. Joshua said we use different last names. So the Jewish lady took a good look and said, 'You sure you not kin?' 'No ma'am. I'm Daniel Jones. This Calvin Jackson. This Matthew Higgins. This Joshua Torch.' She said, 'All right. All right.' Then she got real quiet. 'But you sure do favor!' Walked off talking to herself. 'These people sure do favor!' "

They were quiet as she smoothed the cloth. Cut.

She thought. Of that tiny room. September night. The Reader. She had cried herself sick. Fainted. Found herself surrounded by white. Hospital. Daniel and his brothers came. Sang in wide country voices, softly at her bed. Helped bring her home, when she was better. Helped out with chores. Cooked. Had supper waiting for Angela when she got home. Folded napkin on the table. Glass of water. Long after she was better, they came. Angela got up in the mornings, talking aloud. The boys could give her a hand with this. With that . . .

"You really talented," Matthew said.

"Keep your big eyes off my African Flower!"

"We take you for our sister," Calvin said. "We use to having sisters."

"She really is a flower," Daniel said.

Every Saturday since September, they came. Took her to see the Empire State Building. Statue of Liberty. Botanical gardens. Brooklyn Bridge. Zoo. Aquarium. Planetarium. Museums. They hummed and harmonized quietly in the subway. Sang in the arm of the Statue. In the gardens. Argued race. Talked of home. God. War.

It snowed Saturday night into this Sunday morning. Yet the winter church was packed. Abeba smiled at girls who came dressed. Specially dressed. To see Matthew. Six feet tall. Big eyes and laughing dimples. To watch the way Calvin sported. Throw "Christian" arms around Daniel.

Abeba wore her Christmas dress. Blue velvet. Gold rose pin at neck. Matching hat. Her face shining as the brothers, her brothers came forward, the stars of Men's Day at First Baptist. Two days before Christmas. They stood in dark suits. Collars smooth white. With right foot planted forward, hands cupped, Matthew called out in his wide country voice:

Wasn't that a mighty day!

The brothers answered. Sent Abeba's thoughts home. To Mamma Habblesham. Jackson. Rooster.

Wasn't that a mighty day
When
(Sweetly)
Jesus
Christ was
Born.
Angels
Brought the news
Angels
Brought the news
Angels
Brought the news
When
(Sweetly)
Jesus
Christ was
Born.

The four bundled in coats and rubber boots walked through Brooklyn snow. Brief gusts of wind sprinkled the streets.

"Nothing like New York snow to bring on the quiet." Matthew's voice slightly hoarse.

"It is quiet."

"Real peaceful."

Christmas lights scattered in windows brightened the night hour. Bits of songs hummed in Abeba's head.

Matthew spoke suddenly. "We going to turn off here."

"Good night, Little Sister."

Abeba's heart tumbled as she walked with Daniel. Alone in this private night, alone with light snow-quiet steps. Daniel looked like a boy. His leather hunter's cap fastened under the chin. He said fool around with New York winter and you'll get pneumonia, sure as you're born . . . It had been a mighty day. Men's Day.

They turned through streets, quiet as the other side of thought. The wine-velveteen coat kept her warm. Woolen scarf protected her neck.

"Want to sit on the bench a minute?"

Abeba looked across the street at benches lining the stone wall. Behind that the park filled with snow.

"All right."

He held her elbow as they crossed the street. Then with a wide gloved hand, sent snow flying as he whisked it from the bench, exposed wet wood. Abeba was about to sit when Daniel caught her. Quickly pulled her close and kissed her mouth. His mouth warm and soft. His breath beat against her nose. He begged her, "Will-you-marry-me-just-don't-say-no."

Abeba's heart jumped and tumbled across the snow-quiet world.

"Wedding bring you hard luck," Angela said. "You been a hard-headed child. Going to reap what you sow."

"I could still go to school."

"So man-crazy. I told you last September. No. No. No. No ma'am. You can't marry Daniel Torch."

Abeba awoke. After midnight. One week before the wedding. Struggled to breathe. Sweated. Her lungs strained. Pulled. She sat up. Opened her mouth in the dark. Didn't want to die. Turned to her side. Pulled up. Breathing noisily. Tapped on Angela's door. The ambulance from King's County. The police. Swinging red light. The same men who took her father. Carried her down the steps again. She heard doors open. Angela saying, "She was out in the weather." A hard-headed child. Abeba breathed from the covering over her nose. Rode on her back into the ambulance. Rolled. Her body hungry for the hospital sheet.

Under the plastic tent, she began to relax. Looked at Angela through plastic wrinkles. Comforted by the round face. Stout nose. Full eyes. Maybe she should just go to college. Her whole body seemed opened again. Maybe Daniel would wait.

February second, Abeba dressed in soft white. Barbara Willis, her friend from grade school, maid of honor. Matthew and Calvin stood with Daniel. Reverend Judges, prayerfully, near the three windows. Even Angela had bought a bureau so that Daniel and Abeba could live with her after the wedding. Bought a blue lace dress. Had her golden sandals resoled and prepared herself as mother of the bride. And on that day, the living room with a vase of flowers and a wedding cake. The marriage.

12   They had dressed in the small winter space. Some mornings with conversations. Some in quiet. Washed together. Sang in the evening sunlight of three windows. Content.

Then the blood stopped. Suddenly the doll house with pink walls and fluffy curtains changed. Walls seemed newly crowded. Supper hours cluttered with odd-quick looks. Eyes kept on the plate. Now the summer air was humid with Brooklyn heat. The white doctor had put his fingers inside Abeba's body. Pressed her stomach. Felt her breasts. With metal snippers clipped a tiny bit of flesh to examine for diseases. She ached as winter vanished through short hours. Angela had been so hurt. Daniel disappointed. That was April. Now, in July, a child smaller than her fist, curled in her belly. From pinpoint to ten weeks. The soft cartilage curved and breathing water.

Abeba wiped sweat from her upper lip. At the opened window, she looked like a small girl. Hair parted and braided in fine neat rows. She wiped the sweat trickling through the fine hairs at the temple, looked at the children in the street below who opened fire hydrants. A strong spray of water arched the street. Abeba stroked her belly. All that was left of winter. Her body shuddered with soft beatings in the womb. In her breasts. A tingling in the nipples.

Behind her, Daniel searched, rummaged deep into the closet looking for a book. Abeba heard her mother's footsteps.

"Abeba?"

"Yes, Mommie?"

"I don't want no more babies. You hear me?"

Daniel pulled out of the closet.

"One baby is enough baby."

Daniel yanked the door open. "Repeat that. Just repeat that."

"Need to lock it up!" Angela's moist face spoke close to Daniel's.

"You God? Think you God?"

"Daniel!" Abeba almost screamed. "Don't say anything."

"This my house," Angela said.

"Who pays two-thirds the rent?"

"Don't you bless me out in my house. Brazen. Backwards . . ."

"Mommie!" Abeba wiped her face.

"I'll handle this," Daniel said. "Very well. We'll pack and leave you right here in *your* house."

"I'll take something and knock you in the head," she said.

"Close the door, Daniel."

"I'm not afraid of the Devil."

"Daniel . . ."

He slammed the door with a loud snap that echoed. His voice cracked when he spoke. "She is a devil."

"Why did you open the door?"

"Why? Open the door if I want to. Not let somebody make me keep a door closed."

"You know how she is."

"I've got to get out of here. Hanging around a mother-in-law who wants to butcher my baby."

"She didn't say that."

"Didn't have to say that."

He left. Door slammed. From the window Abeba watched him quick-step through the street. Snap around when water splashed him. Walk on.

"You children not going to leave me with a house full of children."

"Mommie! Why can't you give somebody a chance? Can't you stand to see somebody happy?"

"Don't you fly up in my face! I borned you." She threatened to strike Abeba, then lowered her hand. Spoke in a strange whisper. Turned and left.

Abeba sat suddenly. Repeated Angela's words. This your first baby . . . and last baby . . . Or as God is my Savior, Daniel'll know about you and Uncle C-J.

The street children laughed and splashed in water. Water glistening in soft wooly hair. The evening sun left the streets with shadows. Darkness fell. Abeba stared into street lights. Old years came close as her reflection on the night window. Her mother hummed and sewed in the living room. Out in the night, Daniel walked. Voices in the streets vanished. The palm reader's fire stained her hands. The soft baby shuddered in her womb.

Before dawn, Abeba slept fitfully through nightmares. Awoke abruptly. Baffled by the sun. Surprised that she was fully dressed. Depressed by a troubled dream she could not remember. She heard Angela and Daniel in the kitchen laughing. Laughing! Tossed the light sheet aside and got up just as Daniel came in, laughing.

"What's so funny this morning?"

"It's such a pretty day those few words I had with your mother already forgotten."

"Let's move."

"Move? Where'd you get that idea? You haven't even had breakfast!"

"Are you my friend?"

"I'm your husband."

"Don't make fun of me."

"You do look cute in that wrinkled dress. So angry."

"Stop laughing at me!" She hit the small table. "Stop laughing."

"What's the matter, Beba?" He held her.

She spoke quietly. "I wouldn't be under so much pressure if . . ."

"If what?"

"If . . ."

So many years she wanted to tell someone. Within moments, the words she feared from her mother tumbled from her in a rush that left Daniel asking, "Uncle who?"

"C-J."

"Make a woman out of who?"

"Me."

"You mean he tried to . . ."

"Yes."

"Did he actually?"

"Yes."

He whistled. "But your mother . . ."

"Worked."

"You told her?"

"I told her."

"And?"

"She said empty the basin. He's a nasty man."

"What basin?"

"For the icebox."

"We're not discussing iceboxes."

Abeba quieted. Now threatened by Daniel's tone.

"You have any children?"

"No."

"But you literally slept with this uncle!"

"He slapped me."

"How many times?"

"Slapped me?"

"No, slept!"

"About fifty."

"Fifteen?"

"Fifty."

"Well." He studied her face. "Well. Well. Well. Well."

They were quiet a long time.

"The man you called Daddy was not your daddy. You don't actually have a father."

"I have a father!" Then she said, "I'm sorry."

He said nothing.

"Forgive me?"

"For what? You were fifteen. Your uncle took advantage of you." He got up. Put on his shoes. Very carefully. "Your father was dead." Tucked in his shirt.

"Where you going?"

He suddenly cried out. His voice terrible and strong. Tears rolled down his slim face. Glass flew as he broke jars against the iron radiator. "I'll ram this broken brush through his guts!" He shouted, "Where is he? Where is he?"

"I don't know." She whispered.

Angela knocked. "Can't have all that fussing early in the morning."

"You shut up. Shut up!" He opened and slammed the door. His top lip jerked and trembled. "Why you tell me all this now? Why didn't you come out with all this before we married?"

"It was a bad memory."

"Why didn't you forget it?"

"Mommie said. Mommie said . . ." It came to her quietly, underneath the blood pounding her veins. Angela didn't know exactly everything.

The door slammed. Daniel gone. Abeba's hands shook as she rubbed her arms. And rubbed her arms. You have lovely arms, he said. Beautiful brown eyes. Will you marry me a snow magic night in December. Summer now. Her baby, smaller than her fist, covered its forming face.

13   Night fell on the narrow road. Yet the speeding bus took swift sharp curves that jostled the riders. Passengers' eyes snapped open. Abeba's puffed eyes stared at the dark. She wondered about the life of her baby. During the day the sun-heated bus broiled. Her head itched tight with sweat and she tried to relieve it with the little comb, scratching and scratching until she thought her scalp would bleed. Sharp sunlight cut her eyes. Bounced from bright bumpers of cars along the road. She was nineteen now. Her angry husband slept against the window. His head rolled and jerked. Dream-shouted in his soft-easy mumbling, arguing with her mother. With Uncle C-J. He had gone back to his brothers three weeks. Come again with cheap suitcases. Tickets for home. Ordered her to leave the job now! Come with him now! Or give up being Mrs. Torch. Abeba's body was stiff with pain after two days, two nights riding.

Night now. Someone up front fidgeted with a paper bag. Other eyes closed. Half asleep. It was after midnight. Abeba tried to forget the narrow road. To close her eyes and sleep.

The sign said Welcome to St. Augustine, the Oldest City in America. And, soon after, the bus pulled into a long narrow depot, with an overhead shelter stretched the length of the walk. Across the street, stores. Hotel. Horses and buggies waiting. The clear-blue Florida sky and palm trees.

The bus motor shut down. Abeba and Daniel stepped off. Breathed hot Florida air. Joined a jagged line of riders waiting for baggage. Whale-bus vomited up the rest of its passengers. Vomited up boxes and bags. Had digested three eternal days. Three nights.

Abeba stumbled. Her legs filled with shooting needles. Bladder bursting.

Daniel caught her. "You all right?"

"I'm all right."

They were lonesome here. Nobody to meet them. The walks paved with bright sand glistened. Yet the sun's wattage seemed low.

Daniel spoke as though talking to a distant self. "If I'd a thought to send Mamma and Papa notice, they would have sent Roland with Harris." He looked at her kindly. "Harris is the horse." He seemed lost. Crossed the street. Moved from carriage to carriage shouting. "Oleander Street. Oleander!" Drivers shook their heads. He moved down the line. "Oleander!"

They crowded into a wagon loaded with potatoes, blueberries. A man and his son. The horse walked. Wagon bumped along scenic roads. Into back towns for deliveries. Palm trees, with trunks like elephant's legs, filled the roadside. Bushes with sharp green-yellow leaves. Fat yellow flowers dressed the road. The humble houses.

"You all from New York?"

"Yes."

"It's a terrible winter in New York."

"Yes it is."

"But I hear they's plenty money."

Down one road, Abeba saw a woman sweeping. Something about her familiar. The woman turned and looked up with Daniel's eyes. Had heavy dark lips like Daniel's lips.

Mamma Torch hollered. "Roland! Go get Papa. Tell him come

see Daniel and his bride." She tumbled down the steps. "Lord in the morning." Reached for Abeba, but Papa Torch came running, grabbed her from the buggy. Whooped and sailed her big-bellied body around.

"Easy, Papa," Mamma Torch said. "Easy."

There were so many people.

"These the twins, Michael and Moziah . . . That Roland the youngest brother fussing with the horse. This Yolanda. All right! You going to get slapped!" Mamma Torch hollered at the twins her grandsons who fingered the boxes and bags. "Anybody tell you this for you? So why you messing with it?"

Michael and Moziah, hair cut short to scalp. Dressed in large trousers that swallowed their thin hips, followed into the house. In moments a burst of voices, footsteps brought all Oleander Street to the Torch place. A tangle of arms. Kisses. Long Southern drawls.

"Professor!" They called Daniel. "You done changed color. Talk more like a New York professor."

"This the Girls High graduate."

"That nice."

"Mrs. Abeba Torch."

"How you say her name?"

"Abeba. Almost like 'a-baby' but just where you put that 'bee' put a 'ba.' "

They fell out.

"Means African Flower."

"That real nice."

"You like your African name?"

"Of course."

"She do sound like a schoolteacher." They repeated. "Of course."

Abeba walked in the yard with Mamma Torch. In the moon-lit dark. They stepped through shallow puddles.

"Full moon," Mamma Torch said. "Tide's up." She carried a kerosene lamp for the outhouse.

The rooster walked with them.

"You needn't follow too close." Mamma Torch spoke to him as she spoke to the twins. "Or you're liable to wind up Abeba's coming-home supper." She pointed to a wooden cubicle. "You can do your business here."

The outhouse stench forced Abeba right out. She gathered courage and went in again. Her foot tapped the bucket and thick flies flew up. Fat, filled with waste. Insects covered the walls. Watched her. Abeba hurried to use the pail. Sprinkled lime and came out shaken. Thought briefly of the bright clean toilet at home.

"Roland, go pump some water for your sister-in-law. So she wash her hands and face."

The screeching pump brought Carolina years to life. Memory traded places with reality. Thirteen years ago she hugged Mamma Habblesham. Now her New York mother . . . alone in Brooklyn. St. Augustine. Home-built houses. Raw wood. Small windows without glass. Naked floors and wood stoves.

"Don't leave your good nylons on the bed or in the dresser." Mamma Torch stood by. Watched Abeba wash. "We got flying roaches in Saint Augustine big as a man's thumb. Eat your stockings before day. We keeps our stockings in a jar."

Close to midnight, Daniel closed the bedroom door. Horsehair mattress squeaked when Abeba sat. Undressed. Kerosene lamp threw her bending shadows on the wall. Glowed peaceful light on bare wood floor.

She wondered. In his house, would Daniel love her?

He blew out the light.

"Good night, Abeba." He didn't kiss her.

"Good night." She stretched in the dark. Stretched the sore muscles against the stiff mattress. Shifted her body so her belly would be free. Listened to Daniel snore.

When Abeba awoke, Daniel was up. Out. Room door ajar. Clear Florida sun streamed through the window. She heard Roland outside talking to the horse. Chickens fussing. She stirred and the horsehair mattress squeaked.

"Roland!" Papa Torch hollered.

She heard Roland go running round the side of the house. Moments later, dead silence. Abeba left the room, found the house empty. All doors flung open. Someone hollered in the far distance.

From the front porch, Abeba saw Mamma Torch and Papa Torch halfway down Oleander Street and Roland running hard, chasing Daniel!

Mamma Torch hollered, "Call Bubber, Roland."

Roland shouted as he ran.

Papa Torch not far behind.

Papa Torch, Roland and Bubber struggled with Daniel. They half carried, half pulled him up the porch steps. Muscles in his arms and legs hardened as he fought. He was slippery. Naked.

They wrestled him to a chair.

"Stand back," Daniel shouted. "Back back." His voice so loud, they listened. Mamma Torch tried to throw a cover over his private parts. Neighbors gathered and Daniel stood to greet them. Blanket flopped.

Abeba bent to get it.

"Leave that cover there, girl."

She straightened.

He spoke directly to her. "Answer me this . . ."

Her heart hammered.

"Just answer me this. Why did He say 'Father why hast thou forsaken me?' Well?"

"I . . ."

"Speak up, girl. I don't have all day."

"Rest yourself," Mamma Torch said.

"She's my wife! If I want a little enigma straightened out . . ." He banged the chair and a roach big as a man's thumb crawled out. Stunned. "All right. All right. So why is it we say hell is both a place and a condition?"

Abeba opened her mouth.

But Daniel suddenly sat. Saying, "Wheew! Wheew!" As though he were very hot.

"Get your brother a glass of water, Roland."

"Wheew." He wiped his head.

Abeba brought out a navy blue handkerchief. Wiped his burning head. Handed him the handkerchief.

"I thank you," he said quietly.

Doctor Hodgkins gave Daniel medicine and told him to rest his nerves. Just not to do anything more than walk out. Maybe throw feed to the chickens. Something on that order. But no studying the Bible. No books. Nothing hard. Get plenty of rest.

In days he seemed better. Quiet again. Abeba helped him take medicine. Watched him. Mamma Torch sent Roland with them when they walked out. The neighbors hailed them. Daniel spoke out. "How's everybody?" Abeba's thoughts circled. If she hadn't told him. If her mother hadn't . . . if she didn't have . . . if her father wasn't dead . . . if . . .

She didn't know that Daniel's madness had been traced out

years and life years ago. Before the week was out, he vanished. Found young boys on the other side of town, batting ball. Ran bases. Whooped and hollered until the medicine began to work against him. The sheriff caught him. Tied his hands back. Took him down to the jail to rest him overnight. Stopped by the house on Oleander and told Abeba Daniel was going to a hospital. Tallahoochee. A place way out. Place for folks troubled in mind.

14   How did the sun shine in the mornings? Her husband was gone. Had joined another world. A world where patients took marching steps. Turned slowly, staring inside their broken heads. Opened their mouths and let saliva hang. He sang his song. Beware. Now hailed other patients. "Say!" Eyed visitors. Doctors. Paid sharp attention to small things. Ravels. Flies. The patients fought each other. Daniel fought them. The attendants came through. Bruised Daniel across the left cheek. Slapped him so hard blood blocked sound in one ear.

Abeba felt the side of his face.

He pulled her hand away. Smiled differently. Mouth more slanted. Eyes dilated like big basement windows. Barred.

"What happened!"

"Let's get out of here."

"What happened to your face!"

"They struck me." His tongue lagged in his mouth. His words slightly slurred.

"Who?"

"People who run this place. Take black folks for guinea pigs. Let's go. I've had enough of this foolishness. They pump you full of medicine. Know what they did?"

"What?"

"Had somebody big as an ox. A big black ox sat on my back and let a white doctor jam a needle in my spine. And know what they did when I hollered Oh Lord?"

"What?"

"Laughed. They don't care about Jesus. Take it for a joke. Right after they got the poison in me, I had terrible headaches." He held his temple. His fingers angular. Stiff. "And the pain in my back. Feel right along here." He took her hand and rubbed it along his spine. "Right there. There. Ow! I still feel it. They don't care if you die. Keep you right here. Some of these fellows been here two, three years. Some since they were little boys . . . There's the black ox. This my wife," he told the attendant. "Girls High graduate. Not a dumb brute like you setting your rump on somebody's back co-operating with white folks!"

"He fight too much," the attendant said.

"Let's get out of here. Go get my clothes and let's go home. I've had enough of this foolishness."

Abeba went to sign him out. "I'm Daniel Torch's wife. I want to sign him out."

"Sit down," the doctor said.

"He's been here three weeks and he's worse. His words slur."

The doctor leafed through forms. Handed her papers. "We need your signature. Just sign here." Marked an *x*.

Abeba held the pen, poised to sign.

"That's right. Sign there."

"What's this . . ." Her eye sped over the print.

". . . Consent for shock treatment!"

"Your husband's got deep troubles. He's got memories he needs to forget!" He spoke casually. A fattish white man. Unkempt doctor. Stomach bulging in his white jacket. "He'll get worse and worse unless we do something. Might even kill somebody."

"No!" She ripped the forms. "No! Don't you touch my husband.

He got worse after he came here! We're getting out of this place."
She ran out to tell Daniel. Found him crouched in a corner.
"Daniel!" She pulled his arm. "Let's go home."

He mumbled to himself.

"Please, Daniel. Please. Daniel!"

"I'll stay the night. The crazy folk here'll miss me. Most of them
crazy. See that one there with his trousers unfastened?" He
pointed.

"Please, Daniel! Get up! Get up!"

"He's a lunatic. Certified nut."

"Please, Daniel!" He was getting more strange. She walked off.
Ignored the other patients calling to her.

Outside, Roland stood solemnly with Harris the horse. Didn't
know what to say as Abeba cried all the way back to St. Augustine.

Abeba's spirits lifted when Matthew and Calvin arrived. The sister Loretta drove in from Georgia. Wearing a powder blue suit that
fit in the waist. She had smooth skin and a face something like
Mamma Torch's. Yet different. Her hair combed into fat shining
curls around her face.

In Matthew's new car, they rolled quickly toward the hospital.
Talking. Laughing. The ride faster and smoother than the horse.
Soon the sprawling hospital in sight. Wired fence. They sobered.
Trooped through the day room where patients marched and bab-
bled. Some crouched in corners. Rocking. One roared out. Startled
them. Abeba turned and looked at him. He stared back. She
walked quickly. The strange patient roared. Again.

They hurried down a narrow unpainted hall. Walls marked with
oil stains. Dirt. Turned into the tiny cell-room where Daniel lay in
a crib. His hands tied by the wrists. Strips of old sheets tied his
hands to the railing.

Abeba came close.

His eyes were closed. Lids thin. Bruise on his face slightly healed. Daniel. His thoughts flung far from his body. She cried quietly. As though afraid to disturb him.

The Torch minds were on tiptoe. Examined the tube forced through their brother's nose. They were silent. Understood now. In quick glances, they told each other he would die. Looked long at Daniel. Looked away.

Loretta's arm around Abeba trembled. "Maybe if we talk to him." Loretta spoke more loudly. Didn't sound like herself. "Daniel! Boy, you got a new bride here and a baby on the way what you doing stretched out flat on your back this way?"

"Don't disturb him," Matthew said.

"Disturb him! He hasn't moved a muscle. Not one nerve!"

"Loretta!"

"Been laying up here in the hospital how many weeks now and getting worse and worse . . . Where's the doctor? Think they can treat colored people any which way. I want to see the doctor and demand why my brother's laying up here in bed like a dead man and last I saw him he was talking. Strong and fat . . ."

Matthew took her from the room.

"This is ridiculous." She kept speaking.

Abeba, Calvin, Yolanda, Roland followed. Walked quickly. Shaken. A patient blocked their path. His eyes bulged wet.

"Your husband's a zombie," he told Abeba.

"How he speak so good?" Matthew said.

"You got a cigarette?"

"They could send you home."

"You got a cigarette?"

"We don't smoke."

"Your husband's a zombie."

"He's in a coma," Roland said.

They walked. The patient walked with them.

"You got any . . ."

"Where's the doctor?"

"I definitely want to see the doctor," Loretta said.

"She got cigarettes." He stepped close to Loretta.

Matthew blocked him. Threatened with his eyes. "Now you can act as crazy as you want. But lay a hand on my sister and you'll really learn what crazy is all about."

"Patients not allowed fire," Roland said.

Loretta opened her pocketbook.

"She could light it for me." He took the cigarette. "And she could blow out the match."

In a split second of pure silence, Roland struck a match. The lunatic sucked up quiet fire. Roland's breath quiet, blew out the match. This place. Shadows on floor. Window patterns of wired windows. The smell of sweated patients. This place. Sounds. Light. Daniel down the hall silent. Sick. The images began to separate into dreams. A hundred nights the same dream. Maybe not the whole dream. Just the light here. The small flame. Someone trailing her asking for something. Telling her something over and over. Abeba's mind worked rapidly as the nights surfaced. The dry scraping sound of the match stirred up years of dreams.

"Let's find a doctor," Matthew said.

Abeba looked vaguely through him. Tried to remember the end of that dream.

Home again, she lay down gently . . . slept.

Loretta left. Matthew and Calvin went back to New York. Abeba waited. Time strained through the hours. Marked the curve of her belly and pulled it tight. Put weight in her steps and spread her wide feet. She slept. Awoke abruptly.

The night house quiet. She heard roaches squeeze through cracks. Rubbed the stretched skin of her tremendous belly.

Abeba sat near Daniel. Roland outside the hospital with Harris the horse. It was a hot September day. The horse breathed heavily. The close cell where Daniel lay in the crib, hot. Abeba fanned flies from his nose. From the wet spot on his pants. Daniel's skinny face in half-light. Dried lips. Abeba pulled her sticky dress from her shoulders. Stared through the wall. Her thoughts circled.

"How's my African Flower?"

Her heart pounded.

Daniel looked at her. His eyes opened in the half dark.

"I must have dozed off." He tried to lift his hands.

Abeba cried. Blowing her nose and wiping her eyes. Cried while people came. Patients. Doctors. Roland put his arms around her. Quieted her.

"You were right here when it happened," Roland said.

"I was right here."

"You scared us," he told Daniel, whose watery eyes tried to understand the commotion.

"Scared you!" His voice soft. "Both hands tied?"

Florida prepared for a green Christmas. From the bedroom Abeba heard Mamma Torch in the kitchen. Company came to talk. Sample puddings. Mamma Torch had been to the hotel in town, to the back door of the kitchen where they gave her big bags of bread scraps, a dime a bag, and she made puddings with firm, sweet edges.

Abeba in her room to the back, heard Mamma Torch running.

Chase the clucking chickens. Heard the bones break as she wrung their necks. Three for Christmas dinner.

"It's not for you to touch something dead," Mamma Torch said. "Cause you getting ready to bring life."

Abeba rubbed her milk-swollen breasts. Wished for Daniel. But he was still weak. His mind still swung out of place sometimes. His legs had to get their strength back. She rubbed her breasts. They had long secreted the yellow colostrum. She had to use a glass funnel with a rubber bulb to ease the pressure.

Christmas day. Florida day. The kitchen filled with people. Eating and laughing. Abeba's door opened.

"Why you holding on to your Christmas present so?"

Abeba tried to laugh.

"Let that child out to see what Christmas all about."

They closed her door. Three silly ladies. Joking Florida ladies. She wondered what her mother was doing at home.

Two days after Christmas Abeba's hands and feet began to swell. She listened to the midwife in the kitchen, talk with Mamma Torch. A pain hit her. She screamed.

They ran in. Felt her belly. Looked at her. Went away. Unimpressed by pain that ate a solid circle in her back. Sharpened edge cut the base of her belly. Hours passed. Strings of steel-hot pain laced her belly until new pain wiped out the earlier memory of pain. They rushed to her. Lifted her gown and she gripped Mamma Torch's hand. Screaming. She would die.

"Bear down."

Her mother's words came. What you sow. She screamed. Oh, God. She might die.

"Now."

"Bear down."

Her body would burst. If she could just get through the next moment. She begged Mamma Torch. "Help me." Screamed.

The midwife finally lifted her. Held her body half-sitting. Rubbed her back and belly with a sweet oil. And something pushed lower. And lower. Sploshed out.

Abeba saw the grayish form. She was struck by the limp body dripping blood. The midwife quickly wiped mucus from the small mouth. Put her mouth to the baby's and breathed. Color shot through the tiny body and he cried until the whole earth was bright green. He was the sun that soaked up pain. The morning sun shining while blood flowed between her legs. Abeba's spirit was new. She was a woman now. Aglow as the tiny soft form, washed and wrapped, snuggled in her bosom. Her baby. Hey bop!

Word went out to Daniel. Attendant got the news. Said, "Well, Torch, another little preacher is born."

15   It was a June morning in Brooklyn. Smells of baking bread came from the little shop on Thatford Avenue. The Torch Bakery. More than four years ago, folks watched Abeba and Daniel come from the South with two small boys. Saw her go to the hospital over and over. Carrying pink blanket. Blue. Another blue. Nobody said much till they got the word they trying to build a bakery. Then everybody had something to say. Drunks who woke after noon. People who collected city checks once a month. Children. Casual mothers who served baked beans for breakfast, cold from the can, all discussed this bakery thing.

"Can't no black folks have no bakery."

"Here? Not on Thatford Avenue!"

"War's on."

"Sugar short."

Daniel bought a cake mixer. They got Roland's sugar coupons; he was in the army.

"Black folks don't buy from black folks."

Abeba and Daniel set low-low prices.

"Where they get money to start no business?"

Abeba shopped rummage shops. Pants fifteen cents. Shoes ten cents. A quarter. Children slept on flour bag sheets. Drank canned milk. Had meat only Sundays.

"They liable to call the husband to fight."

He had a hospital record.

Abeba watched the man who rolled back his sleeves nine summers ago, who sang "Beware," who read the history of Africa and loved Sundiata, roll back his sleeves, again. Work ten hours in the Brooklyn Navy Yard. Come home. Saw wood, plaster and paint walls, building bakery. Buy bright steel bowls. Decorator's set. Bread slicer.

"Rats eat all the bread," Angela prophesied.

Angela had remarried. Lived in a steam-heated apartment. Fixed up her place with new refrigerator. Fancy dishes. Came once a week to spoil her grandchildren. To tell Daniel put a lock on it. Remind him that our people good for nothing but making babies. Tell Abeba that she borned her and to complain about the cold water flat.

Angela squeezed her way from front to back complaining about boxes. Asked Jesus to help her. Came to the second bedroom where curtains hanging on a string hid Abeba and Daniel's bed. Begged the Lord for Mercy. She stepped into the kitchen. Abeba watching. For years, Angela looked at the kitchen floor with fresh horror. Floor had been blue with red and yellow flowers. Most of the color mopped off. Wall behind the stove painted silver. Kitchen supposed to be white. Boxes off to one corner. Blackboard. Angela stood before the kitchen board, a big board lined with musical staffs. Notes for tenor, soprano, alto. The solfeggio written under each note. A *black* board in a kitchen. She reminded Daniel that he was backward. Told Abeba that she had a good education and asked Jesus to have mercy on her daughter without the backbone. And was finally silent when she saw the horseshoe wedged through the broken places in the back door to lock it shut.

"Can't have bakery here," Angela said. "Rats eat the bread. Rats in Brownsville big as the cats."

They were terrible rats. Walked off with bacon and sweet candy tied to small traps. Daniel had to get rat-sized traps strong enough to snap a small child's hand. Abeba stuffed cardboard at the base of cribs so rats wouldn't jump through the slats and bite her babies. Attracted to the sweet smell of babies' urine. She sensed them waiting in the dark. Heard them on the night floor. Her nerves a net triggered when they set foot near the crib.

Daniel stuffed rags into cracks beneath the bakery door.

Abeba's face was thoughtful as the electric beater whipped a dozen egg whites. Her daughter, five years old, stood on a chair. Watched.

"Is that about right?"

"Yes, Kora."

"That's for meringue?"

"Yes, Kora."

Beater stopped. Abeba splashed white peaks onto smooth lemon filling in rich brown crusts.

"Can I do some?"

Abeba held Kora's small waist as she splooshed white topping. Abeba's brown eyes content. "That's good."

The Torch bakery burst with summer sun. Golden bread. Behind her Daniel, in tall hat, starched white, stepped and turned. The cake mixer the children called the elephant, with its long gray mixing stem, hummed its catchy rhythm. Rasser-rasser-rasser-rack. Rasser-rasser-rasser-rack. Machine, floor vibrated. Joshua, younger than Kora, helped his older brother Askia-Touré by catching the peels as they unravelled from apples. Askia looked like an elf. Six and a half. Front tooth missing. He plugged apples on the machine. Turned the handle and it spit out the core. He peeked through the empty space. Let his brother Joshua look through.

Put the apple in the bowl. Started on another. He wore knickers. Complained. Called the fifteen cents' bargain "chicken pants." When Abeba said these are riding pants, he hollered "I don't have a horse!" And then complained. The children teased him. Ask Askia. Ask Askia. Abeba made him proud. Told him Askia was the finest scholar in the world. And he had been happy.

In moments, Daniel-Jr's running footsteps heard through the commotion made everyone look up.

"The short hand is off the eight," he breathed heavily, "and the long hand is on the nine!"

Kora stared at him. Askia-Touré. Joshua. The baby Asa. Daniel-Jr had run down the street where dogs rummaging through trash lifted their heads to watch. Peeked into the window. Saw the candy store electric clock. Came running back with the time.

"It's forty-five after eight."

Their eyes narrowed.

"It's a quarter to nine."

Such magic. To tell the time three ways! They were jealous. Proud.

"Thank you, Daniel-Jr." Abeba turned the metal piece, wound the clock tight. The ticking smothered by the cake mixer's rasser-rasser.

"Fifteen minutes till opening," Daniel said. He stepped to the work table. Abeba made space. Pulled Kora back.

Daniel worked long rolls of ripe dough. Both arms stretched full length. In each hand rolls budded by the dozens and with machinelike flurry he placed them in even rows on pans waiting, oiled and floured. Zing. Into oven. Door closed. He turned. Hot butter. Sugared spices poured over even lumps of apples. Second crust tossed, draped, trimmed. Baker's magic. He quick-stepped through the house. To the kitchen where summer fell through back windows. Joshua, three years old, shot after him.

"Papa!"

Kora stood, watching. Hand on tiny hip.

"Papa!"

"That Joshua sure loves to punch the dough!" Kora said.

"Can I punch down the dough?"

"Stand back, son."

Daniel's strong arm punched. Fermented smells swooshed into the June air. He let Joshua help.

"One more rising," he called to Abeba. Stopped the cake mixer. Back in the shop pulled bright golden cakes from the oven. Sunlight splashed through the big window. Fell across his face. Black and smooth, set off by the white cap.

Abeba dipped the pastry brush in warm butter. Sploshed oil over dough.

Eight years ago, he hadn't moved for close to thirty Florida nights. Eight years ago, he couldn't get one straight thought. But he built this bakery. The walls. You should have seen these walls four years ago, now smooth as unruffled lakes. Bright sun bounced off icing white walls. Crystal clear counters.

In the quiet, Daniel layered chocolate cake. Covered with thick servings of icing. In even strokes, caught drippings from the top. Smoothed sides.

Abeba looked into his face. Daniel Torch. Her husband, intent . . . He was a bush with a new shoot.

Back in the kitchen, Abeba set tin pans of milk before Daniel-Jr, Askia-Touré, Kora, Joshua.

Daniel came through with hot cake. Quickly cut and laid a smoking portion near each plate.

"Thank you, sir."

"Welcome."

"Thank you, sir."

"Welcome."

"Thank you, sir."

"Welcome."

"Thank you, sir."

"Welcome."

He left. And the front door's tinkle-tinkle announced the first customer. Another day started.

She was twenty-seven now. Very different from the little girl who married. Just nineteen. So lost in Florida eight years ago. So surprised by the human being who splashed out of her. Yet seemed so new to her. Abeba's eyes filled with years of thought as the children ate. Slurped milk from spoons. Ate hot vanilla cake.

Nine years of marriage. Seemed like ninety. Their lives in St. Augustine. Maryland. Back to Brooklyn. They had seen so much sickness. Thefts. Near deaths . . . Daniel-Jr just two. Sitting outside in his stroller. The noise! Something heavy falling through the fire escape. Clothes iron hit the dirt. Fell two inches from his face. "It slipped," the owner said. "Sorry." Picked up her iron and went back upstairs.

"Mamma!"

"Yes, Kora."

"Won't I start school in September?"

"Yes."

"And Askia has to hold my hand."

"You're a girl."

"Of course she's a girl. She's your sister."

"And Grandmother says she'll buy me a new dress so I'll look decent."

"Finish your breakfast," Abeba said.

Bread rises fast on summer mornings. The sun rose full. Bakery bells brought customers. Abeba hummed as she washed and oiled Asa who wiggled his long feet. Caught her ear when she bent to kiss him.

"This is the baker-man's son."

Asa's black eyes sparkled.

"This is Mamma's sweet little boy."

16 The sign outside Public School 84 announced:

A *Neighbourhood play*
NEBUCHADNEZZAR AND
THE YOUNG MAN DANIEL
by Mrs. Abeba Lavoisier Torch

Kora had told classmates her mother wrote the play. They had been suspicious. Even with the coincidence of same last names. But the day after Thanksgiving, Brownsville neighbors gathered in the school yard. They had heard about this play since school started. About Ohio playing a king. Ain't that something. Ohio never been off the stoop and he the king playing crazy. He was crazy sure enough.

They had come to the bakery and asked Abeba.

"You write that play?"

"Yes."

"You say I come by myself I got to pay fifty cents, but I bring someone with me, we both get in for a quarter?"

"Yes."

"I give you fifty cents now. Bring someone. And at the door you give me back a quarter?"

"Yes."

"Can't beat that."

Voices were heard in the early autumn.

"What you doing day after Thanksgiving?"

"Nothing, man."

"Want to make a dime?"

"Doing what?"

"Come on with me to the show. I give you a dime."

Brownsville neighbors gathered in the hundreds. Marched through brown metal doors where Abeba and four neighbors collected tickets.

"This my partner."

She gave back a quarter.

Some single people waited for a quarter. Didn't know they had to have somebody with them. They ducked back into the streets hollering.

"Come see Ohio make a fool of hisself."

"What?"

"You know the people what got a bakery on Thatford?"

The auditorium at P.S. 84 was packed close when the lights went down. Noise rushed up. Cheers filled the room. Abeba left one roll of quarters at the door with her neighbors. Found her way down the dark aisle through the clapping.

"Over here, Mamma." The children called to her. The dark settled.

Cathleen Jones, who was twelve and big for her age, stepped on stage, draped in fresh white cloth:

"*Tonight, the Brownsville Players would like to present* Nebuchadnezzar and the Young Man Daniel. *The part of the king will be played by Robes Smith, known as Ohio . . . The Young Man Daniel will be played by Reverend Daniel.*"

In the dark, Abeba held the small hands.

"*Nebuchadnezzar was a evil king. He tried to burn three boys in the fiery furnace.*"

"Shadrach, Meshach and Abednego," someone called.

"Shut up!"

She continued, "*Shadrach, Meshach and Abednego. He was a strong, tall king whom everybody feared.*"

The curtain pulled back.

The collective dark astonished by the brilliant color. Oaktag paintings. The court. Throne royal "velvet" and bright gold. Ohio dressed in full paper robe. Glowing crown and fake beard, sat tall. His guards, Big John and Clyde, stood near him.

Whistles.

"You doing it man."

"Shut up you guys."

"*I've had a dream which troubles me.*" The king held his head. "*It spoils my days and spoils my nights. It is in my bread. In every cup I drink.*"

Abeba squeezed the small hands.

"*I will send for the magicians to interpret my dream.*"

The magicians tramped on stage. Dressed in tall hats. Wide robes. Carried special rods. Chased each other with paper snakes.

The audience clapped. Laughed.

They poured clear water. It turned to blood.

"Work that magic," someone hollered.

"I like this play," Kora whispered.

The king roared. "*Enough!*" Shook the ceiling. "*And my dream?*"

"*Umh . . . uh . . .*" The magicians crowded close together.

"They scared now."

"Quiet, man."

"That crazy king'll burn 'em."

"Like he did the Hebrew dudes."

"You are meat for the lions!"

"What I tell you."

"Mamma, someone keeps talking."

"It's all right. Papa will be out soon."

"Call the astrologers."

Matthew led the astrologers on stage. Their faces bearded. Their black robes covered with silver stars and moons. They held paper telescopes to their eyes. Stared into the audience sky dark.

"Can't see a damn thing. Black faces in the dark."

Laughs.

"My dream!" shouted the king.

"Your dream? O King, we know the sky . . ."

"It's Uncle Matt." Joshua tugged Abeba. "It's Uncle Matt."

"Yes."

"We know the stars. But oh, King, we know not your dream."

"Be off."

A great noise was heard to the left.

"Uh-uh!"

The Chaldeans entered fighting.

"Here comes Uncle Calvin," Askia cried.

"I know."

They fought with paper swords. Jumped and turned.

"Mess that mother up."

"Don't cuss in here man. Kids in here."

"And my dream?"

"Your dream?" The Chaldeans looked at one another. Ohio the king opened his mouth. Before he hollered, the Chaldeans vanished.

The soothsayers came. Black cat jumped from the basket. Sniffed the crystal ball.

"It's a real cat!"

"Ho, ho, ho. Look at that cat."

"*You are those who communicate with the dead. Surely you will know the dream.*"

"*We know not the dream.*"

They gathered the cat. Left.

"*There was a young man named Daniel . . .*" The king thought aloud. "*Given to fasting and prayer. Who does not eat the king's meat or drink the king's wine. Send for this man.*"

Daniel walked on. Wearing a short wrap. Cardboard sword at his side.

"*It is said you interpret dreams.*"

Daniel took a deep, sweeping bow.

The audience clapped. Laughing.

Daniel glanced around. His eyebrows lifted. This *is* the king. I'm just giving him a proper respect. Wordless, he took a second deep bow and the audience fell out. Settled.

The king spoke, "*I, Nebuchadnezzar, dreamed of a tall tree, in the middle of the earth. It grew to touch the sky. Its branches covered the earth.*" Ohio the king looked at Daniel the Daniel. He walked about. "*Its leaves were broad.*" His hands stretched. "*Its fruit full sweet.*"

Abeba wiped tears. Watched smiling.

"*Then in the dream a watchman from heaven cried, 'Cut down the tree. Cut down the tree. Leave the root, but cut the tree.'*"

Daniel stood silent.

Audience waited.

Lights fell on Daniel's slim legs. The firm muscles of his arms. At his side, the cardboard sword.

"*O King, it gives me great sadness to say . . .*" He paused. "*You are the tree!*"

Nebuchadnezzar came toward him.

"You will be cut down." Daniel backed off. *"And eat grass like wild oxen, because you know not God."*

Nebuchadnezzar tumbled against his throne. Crawled through the stage light. Daniel checked him with the sword. Guards tried to help. Chaldeans. Astronomers. Soothsayers and magicians rushed on stage. Fed him grass.

Cathleen the narrator came on stage.

"The day Nebuchadnezzar remembered God, his reason returned. And he stood as a man again of sound mind, because he had heard the words of the young man Daniel. The End."

Applause came through the dark. Solid. With shouts and whistles. The Brownsville Players bowing. Abeba's face glowed. She clapped. The new baby inside her had already heard her father's voice. Her mother clapping. Laughing.

17 Abeba pulled the blanket from the baby's sleeping face. Soft cheeks. Tiny hands closed. She smiled at her husband.

"She is a beauty."

Their second daughter sighed. Slept. She was the one who poked her mother in the ribs. Who hid in the dark, comforted by water. Who heard her father's voice, and laughed with the audience outside. For months Abeba felt her pelvis broaden. Stretch wider. Wider. Now look at those tiny legs. Shaped just like Angela's. Soft knees. Scaly skin, oiled.

"Let's call her Little Angela."

The baby's hands flew into the air. Cake machine startled her. Abeba rocked her. Held the soft weight nestled against her bosom. She forgot the sore places. Hospital mirrors. White coats. Hours of labor. Nurses. Screaming mothers.

The little girl opened her eyes. Smiled at Abeba.

"Now that was something," Daniel said. "That was something."

"You have a new sister," Abeba told the children.

"For real?" Kora peeked at the tiny face.

"How'd we do that?" Askia-Touré's front teeth had grown in.

Angela was tickled. Spoke to everyone on Thatford.

"They named the new one after me."

"You deserves it."

"Father so stubborn and backward I didn't think he had it in him. But praise the Lord they named the little one after me. Looks just like me."

She came and sat with her granddaughter. Hummed and smiled over her. It seemed no time before Little-Angela grew. Admired her older sisters and brothers who talked so easily. Walked. Ran. She stood with them to sing every evening. Her face round like her grandmother's. Eyes filled with sweet laughter. The brothers kissed her. Her sister. Strangers stopped in the streets. Gave her a nickel. Nurses at the clinic carried her, kissed her. Little-Angela smiled. Her new teeth bright. Her mouth smelling of milk.

She grew and the bakery grew. The elephant hummed its catchy rhythm. Rasser-rasser-rasser-rack. Bakery bells tinkled. Baking bread filled the rooms. Winter. Summer. She toddled to the front where Daniel called, "Stand back."

"That cake most done?"

"Just about."

"Oh."

She ran after Daniel. He turned suddenly, caught her up in the air. Rubbed his face in her stomach until she laughed and kicked. Holding onto his head. Squeezing the tall hat.

She ran after him into the kitchen. Breathless. "Papa. Can I punch down the dough?"

He lifted her. Laughing as her tiny fist tapped the surface. "All right. Let Papa handle this."

Daniel punched and air swooshed, fermented smells filled the kitchen.

"Wow!" She clapped.

On Little-Angela's second birthday, Daniel signed a lease for a larger store. The children had eaten birthday cake. Little-Angela had sung the birthday song over and over. Her grandmother helping her, until exhausted, she slept, long before night.

It was night now. Abeba thought she would tell Daniel their seventh child was taking form.

"That was a happy little girl." Daniel undressed.

"Yes."

"Seems to come natural to her."

"Hope Mommie doesn't spoil her . . ." Abeba paused. Heard footsteps. Urgent. Quick.

They pulled on robes. Hurried to unbar the kitchen door.

"Matthew!" His face looked terrible.

"Some tragedy happened."

"What?"

"Calvin's in jail."

"What?"

"I just went on down to Penn Station to meet him and I see him coming out hands tied behind his back. I took it for a joke. But it wasn't no joke. All I could get out of him was he stopped for a soda. And naturally had to put his bag down. He wasn't paying much attention to nothing. Picked up his bag again and next thing the detectives come over. He looked and saw the bag wasn't his. He said this not my bag. And naturally they just took him on down to the station house."

"You followed."

"Yeah. I followed. Asked them what the charge. They said he raped and murdered a white woman."

Daniel laughed. Bitter. "How a man just get into town, not long enough to drink a little soda have so much time for rape and murder!"

"I said officer, this man just got here. This my brother."

"He had his ticket?"

"No. It was in the other bag."

Daniel whistled. Held the side of his head.

Abeba pulled her robe tighter. "What's the bail?"

"Won't set no bail."

"Call everyone," Abeba said. "Loretta. Yolanda. Roland. Mamma Torch. Papa Torch. Start tonight."

Little-Angela ran after her father. He was dressed in a dark suit. Shirt. Tie. He didn't see her.

"How do I look?"

Abeba brushed his collar. Touched his tie. "Fine." She felt his pressure rising. Strain showed in his face.

"Expecting two deliveries today."

"Okay."

Uncle Matt's horn tooted.

"I'm off."

"God is with you," Abeba said.

The children followed her to the front. It was eight in the morning. The Torch sisters and brothers waved from the car. Car rolled off for the second week of court. Abeba stood, slip hanging. Her head wrapped in a scarf. Her eyes aching.

"Where's Joshua?" she asked suddenly.

"Under the bed."

She called him. "Joshua! This is no time to play."

He crawled out. "But I'm hiding from the police mans, though. So they won't put me in the jailhouse like they did Uncle Calvin."

"Who told you that?"

"Grandmother."

Late that afternoon, Angela found Abeba in the kitchen.

"Well, when they going to let Calvin out that jailhouse?"

The hall filled with footsteps. Daniel. Matthew. Loretta. Roland. Yolanda. Their faces thin.

"How'd it go?"

They sat. Silent. Loretta opened her coat. The collar with fox head and feet frightened Joshua who stood between his grandmother's legs.

"Twelve men on the jury," Angela said.

"Practically got his Ph.D.," Matthew said.

"Means nothing."

"In divinity! I'm talking about preaching."

"You think the judge crazy about Jesus?"

"They use the Bible."

"In God we trust, written in big letters."

"Lawyers are expensive!" Loretta said. "Had to give him eight hundred from the start."

"But he's good."

"They like to pick out a volunteer lawyer for poor folks."

"He going to tell you plead guilty. Throw yourself on the mercy of the court."

"Next thing," Daniel said, "Judge holler, 'May the Lord have mercy on your soul.' "

"Mercy Jesus." Angela patted her foot. "Need to let Calvin out that jail so he preach to some of these no good men sit around all day. All night. Drink. Cuss. Make mischief. Mercy Jesus."

"Grandmother."

"What Grandmother's baby want?"

"Will Uncle Calvin be electrocuted for rake and murder?"

Daniel grabbed Askia-Touré. "You so grown. You so grown." He threw him to the floor. Struck him with his hands. Grabbed a leather strap from the wall. "So grown!" Ripped his pants down and struck the bared hips.

Kora cried, screaming.

"Daniel!" Everyone called him.

"That's enough."

"Your nerves bad." Angela stood to stop him. "You beat that baby because your nerves bad."

Daniel looked at Angela. Mad.

"Leave, Mommie," Abeba warned.

"I borned you."

"We got court tomorrow!" Matthew shouted. "We all going to leave."

He took Angela's shoulders.

"Be by in the morning."

The little ones didn't sleep. Little-Angela put her arms around Kora who cried. Who wouldn't stop crying. Askia-Touré and Daniel Jr lay quietly in bed. Joshua and Asa side by side on their cot.

"Come to bed early tonight, Daniel."

"Got customers tomorrow." Poured sugar and soft butter into the mixer. Cracked a dozen eggs.

"Let's close shop tomorrow."

"We just paid three hundred for the lawyer. Remember?"

"I know."

"Got a big family to feed."

"I know."

He started the machine. The rasser-rasser-rasser-rack boomed in her head.

"So work with me," he shouted.

"I'm trying, Daniel!" She shouted back. Lowered her voice. The children awake. Listening. "I'm trying."

Was it only a week later? The Torches gathered in the crowded kitchen. Prayed. And sang in full harmony. Songs from lean-fasting bodies rang clear. Smooth. The song attracted the feet of children who would remember this voice. This day of icy-bright sun when Uncle Calvin came home. Free. Because his sisters and brothers fasted, drank water only, for three weeks. Abeba only milk.

Little-Angela stepped close to her father who lifted her up. Sat her on his knee. And kept singing.

18   It was Thursday, Brooklyn-Queens day. A bright-bright morning. Something told her don't leave the house today. But Abeba had dressed, ready for her prenatal check-up.

"I'll be back in two hours," she told Daniel.

"All right." He scraped the burnt bottom from cakes. Cakes had been burning one or two times a day. His hands and arms had fresh burns.

"Don't try to sell that one."

He gave her a sharp Tallahoochee look.

Madness eats in a hurry. His head a dry ceiling, too close to flame.

"You got an appointment, don't you?"

"Yes." Her heart pounded. Close to a month he worried over Calvin. Four hours sleep. Fasting. In court all day. Up cooking half the night. It came to her again. Don't leave this house today.

"Well, are you going? Or you going to stand there dreaming?"

"I'm going."

Within the hour, cakes blackened. Burnt smell seeped into the streets.

Little-Angela came through the smoke coughing.

"Papa. That cake is all burnt."

"Stand back."

She held his apron. Coughed.

"Stand back."

His voice so loud, she froze.

"You not going to listen to your Papa?"

He slapped her. Knocked her to the floor. She tried to scramble up and he slapped her again. Kora came running. She was next.

"All you children been asking for a whipping." He hunted them. Daniel-Jr. Askia-Touré. Joshua. Asa. Beat them.

There was a strained quiet. Heavy smell of smoke when Abeba got back. Two hours later. Rushed into the kitchen and found the children huddled together. Bruised. Bloody. The little table filled with sodas. Cake. Pie.

Their swollen faces watched her.

A strange animal sound escaped her body. She rushed to Little-Angela. One eye closed. Welts streaked her face. Kora, mouth swollen. Cut. Asa, forehead bruised. Daniel-Jr, eyes red. Askia-Touré, lip cut, rubbed his leg. Joshua, shirt soaked in blood.

"His nose was bleeding." Daniel-Jr apologized for his father. "But it stopped now."

Dry blood caked the tiny nostril.

Abeba lifted Little-Angela, carried her to the front steps. The others followed, holding on to her. She stood with her beaten children. Her mind flying.

"Mrs. Torch!"

"What happened?"

Neighbors gathered.

"Goddamn!"

"Daniel-Jr!" They spoke to the oldest son. "What happened to your face?"

Abeba felt a shrill scream rising when someone said, "The uncle here."

Matthew pulled up in his blue car.

Crowd cleared.

He carried Askia-Touré. Helped settle the children in the back of the car. Went to the shop with Abeba.

Daniel decorated lopsided cakes. All burnt. Squeezed the canvas bag and sloppy letters spurted out a watery-pink mess. His apron smeared with burnt crumbs. Soiled with blood.

"What have you done to the children?" Abeba asked in a low-low voice.

Daniel decorated cakes.

She screamed. "Stop it!" Snatched his hat. "Take off that hat." Knocked cakes from the table. Trampled them.

Daniel came toward her.

Matthew grabbed him. Iron-locked his arms around him.

"She's my wife."

"You done enough harm for one day. Come by to take the kids to see the parade and Little-Angela eye closed up. Askia-Touré can't walk . . ."

Abeba broke and cried.

Daniel went to the car with his brother.

"You almost killed the children," Abeba said days later.

"I lost control."

"What happened?"

"Something snapped. Looked like I needed space and Little-Angela crowding me out, well I just let her have it. Kora came next and she was next. I looked for the others. Then I came to myself . . ."

"You almost killed them. You have to rest here."

"How long?"

"Doctor says three months. You have to take medicine for a year. No need to have money to buy a new house if the children are dead."

"God knows I'd rather die first."

"What got into Papa?" Kora asked.

"Papa has high blood pressure."

"What's high blood pressure?" Askia-Touré asked.

"That's when the heart works too hard to pump the blood because the vessels are tight. It means there's too much tension."

"Oh."

"Papa crazy, crazy, crazy!" Angela said.

"Isn't your heart the size of your fist?" Dan-Jr asked.

"That's right."

"And capillaries are real thin."

Abeba wiped Dan-Jr's forehead. He read too many books.

"This thin?" Joshua measured a small space between his thumb and forefinger.

"Much thinner, son. Much thinner."

"Will Papa die?" Askia-Touré asked.

"What? No, son. Papa won't die."

Matthew came by every evening. Set up the cake mixer. The rasser-rasser had a lonesome sound.

"You boys help your mother peel those potatoes."

He surprised them. Uncle Matt giving orders. They listened.

Little-Angela held his apron and followed him through the house.

Abeba rolled out the dough. Slowly filled pans with rows of

buns. Not so pretty as Daniel's. But the rolls were selling. Customers came by. Asked after Daniel.

"How's your husband?"

"Better, thank you."

"When you going to write another play?"

"Soon."

19   The other day someone come around looking for the Torch Bakery. Different ones tell him you must of been away over a year now. No more Torch Bakery. Torch Church. Old sign scraped off the window. Now:

> God's Children's Baptist Church
> Rev. D. A. Torch   Pastor

Printed in gold and white. Blackboard in window had Sunday text printed in Daniel's hand:

> The wolf also shall dwell with the lamb, and the leopard shall lie down with the kid; and the calf and the young lion and the fatling together; and a little child shall lead them.
>
> ISAIAH 11:6

Topic: A Better Day

Folks on Thatford read the sign. Said we sure do need a better day. We need something better than what we got. Ain't got nothing.

Inside, the bakery counters, bread slicer, big silver oven, all sold. Cake mixer, and whatsoever had to do with baking, cleared out. They got a upright piano now. Forty to fifty folding chairs. Pulpit. During the week the front room's for Daniel-Jr and Askia-Touré. Sunday morning, they fold the bed. Sweep out the room and set up chairs. Ten o'clock, doors open for Sunday school. All those twelve to fourteen sit to the left. They the Advanced. Daniel teaches them. Abeba got the Intermediates over to the right, near the piano. All those eight through eleven. Smack in the middle, the little ones. The Beginners can't do no more than mumble and sleep. Repeat what Matthew say and get up going back and forth to the bathroom. Matthew just married. Darlene his pretty wife sit in the back and admire him.

"How many in here afraid of snakes? Hold up your hand."
Hands went up.
"You don't have to be afraid of snakes," Daniel told the Advanced.
"Or lions."
The Advanced were interested.
"Not even Timothy who sucks his thumb even though he's a big boy going on twelve why you suck your thumb Timothy?" He went on. "You not afraid, nothing bothers you. You afraid, you attract things to you every time. Let's go over that again."
Daniel fasted once a week. Rose at five in the morning. Spent one hour in meditation and prayer. Worked eight hours in the kitchen at the telephone company. Took his medicine.
"I'd kill the lion," Timothy said.
"No," Daniel said.
"Because he has his good points," Daniel-Jr said. He was younger than the other Advanced. But wiser.
"That's right."
"He's brave."

"Very good, son."
"But he eats up the sheep!" Askia-Touré reminded them.
"Are we just talking about literal lions?"
"Figurative," Daniel-Jr said.

"Repeat after me . . . Suffer the little children."
The Beginners mumbled.
"To come unto Me."
They mumbled again.
"I got to pee, Mr. Torch."
"Help her to the bathroom."
One Beginner helped another.
"And forbid . . ."
Matthew's wife, Darlene, smiled.
"Them not . . ."

"Sister Torch, may I read?"
"Yes, Clarissa."
"And the . . . what's that word?"
"Leopard."
"Leopard. Shall lie . . . what's that word?"
Kora watched the weak Intermediate.
"Down."
"Down."

"Now. What you like about the leopard?" Daniel asked the
Advanced.

Summer Saturdays, they trooped through the streets.
"I see you got your army."
"All them yours?"

"Yes."

"God bless you. God bless you."

Daniel carried the baby Arthur Lavoisier. Heavy shopping bags.

They boarded the bus. The driver desperate to keep track of fares. Daniel dropped in a handful of nickels. Went to the back where the family sat.

At the park, they put down their bundles. Let go each other's hands and ran. Chased squirrels. Last-tagged and ran with feet hungry for open spaces. They filled a long picnic table. Ate baloney and cheese sandwiches on store-bought bread. Drank cold cherry ade until their mouths were cold and sweet.

Daniel took his pills. Ate his food.

Abeba watched the wind-ruffled trees. Grass stretched to a distance. Neat green. The children quiet and satisfied. There would be a better day.

20   "This is it, African Flower."

The moving men worked like ants. Carried out boxes. Shabby furniture that first week of spring. March.

"Didn't know four rooms could hold so much."

"Seven years," Daniel reminded her.

The Brownsville neighbors sat on stoops. Looking.

"I'll miss them."

The sun was shining on the liquor signs. Beer advertised on four corners.

The junkman hollered. Rang his iron bell. His horse stopped.

The children ran up to the horse who twitched his ears. Stared into his eyes.

"We have enough room at the new place," Daniel said. "We could get them a horse."

"This the last," the mover told them.

Abeba went into the house for a final look. Alone. The empty rooms, suddenly bigger. There had been bitter times and special times. Times she looked up to see Little-Angela thoughtful. Sucking her gums, feeling with soft tongue the edge of a new tooth. Here, in this place, Asa's soft legs straightened. Took a few steps. Flopped over. Christmas. Kora, Daniel-Jr, Askia-Touré, Joshua tumbled through the house. How come Santa Claus didn't bring us a new refrigerator? Askia-Touré asked. But they were happy spinning tops that hummed and swirled colors. They blew horns, had tea parties, ran trains. Children soak up the world around them. Sprinkles of water. Sea-smells of crabs. Want to ride only a moving horse on the Merry-Go-Round. Who was it so humiliated by rides on the stationary horse? Asa? Joshua?

Daniel catered Long Island clubs. Out till all hours Saturday nights. Earned some nights more than he did in a week.

Abeba heard Daniel's quick steps in the hall. Coming to get her.

"There you are. Please don't get sentimental over these infested walls."

She took his arm.

"Let's go, African Flower."

After Brooklyn's tall buildings, Long Island houses look low. Like the walls cut away to let down the sun. The sky comes close to every house. Wide streets planted with lots of trees. The family had been squeezed together in Matthew's car, but no one complained. He parked before the house with three gates. The children sat still. It seemed they were visiting. Would have to be on their best behavior or feel the strap when they got back to Brooklyn.

"Come on," Abeba said.

They got out, careful. Stood on the sidewalk before the long picket fence. Brown and white.

"This our house?"

"Yes."

They looked up. Three stories. Walked through the middle gate. Down the paved walk that went around the house and along front and back yards.

"Shall we go in?"

"Yes."

They followed each other close. Felt the beautiful papered walls.

Bright kitchen print. Walked over polished floors. Up the steps. Opened doors.

"You big boys take this room."

"Yes sir."

"Asa and Joshua in here."

"Yes sir."

"Kora and Little-Angela, here."

"Yes sir."

They walked carefully. Looked from twenty-eight windows. Wondered at the big yard below and ran out into it. Ran under the grapevines that broke into new green leaves.

Wind ruffled the shaggy grass, thick with weeds. Sunlight splashed their upturned faces. Abeba's brown eyes new as the spring. She had seen this place before. Every room. She remembered the March light. The feel of this wind in so many years of dreams. This house. What they had struggled for so desperately had been quietly waiting.

"Plenty room for two pianos," Daniel said.

"It's good to teach the children."

"You're just thirty-one. Plenty time for a career." Then he said what he always said. "Look at Grandma Moses."

21   "I know Abeba Torch when she was Abeba Lavoisier playing down at the church while her mother sing."

"That so?"

"Oh, yeah. I known her mother when she first come to New
York when she was Angela Williams. Then she marry Arthur
Lavoisier. Arthur died and she married almost twenty years ago.
Marry Linsay. And he died."

"That so."

"Honey?" Grandma Hattie squeezed her cane. "This ain't going
to be no Easter you likely to forget. Look at the peoples coming in."

"This some crowd."

"First Baptist use to be couldn't hold all this crowd. Four years
ago they tore out the ceiling. Two walls. Built it up."

They looked around. New balcony filled with Easter hats. Boys
and girls in Easter clothes. Choir lofts. Fine and large organ pipes
gleamed from ceiling to floor. The April sun high. Fell through
stained glass windows. Brown wood polished bright, framed pan-
els painted fresh blue. Hundreds of Easter lilies glistened in baskets with white bows, set at the foot of the pulpit.

"It's beautiful."

"Reverend Judges asked Angela see could she get the children
to come from Long Island to give a program for First Baptist. Bring
her fifteen children."

"What? What you say Grandma Hattie?"

"Fifteen. You'd a never told me that Abeba Lavoisier was going to have no fifteen children."

"What! She planning to have more?"

"No. She can't have no more. They took the womb."

"They took the womb! Umm hum. I don't guess she wanted no more, do you? It's something you don't hear much in this day and age. Especially somebody that got a good education."

"She didn't waste it. She in the college now. And every one of the children smart."

Grandma spotted Angela over the faces. Hats. Waved.

Angela waved. Hugged and kissed the baby, Osei.

Four choirs filled the upper lofts.

The church became quiet.

Abeba. Dressed in African print rich in earth-brown patterns, green vines, went to the piano. Daniel followed in a black and gold dashiki.

He bent and put an arm around her.

"I'm going to go sit next to the 'lion.' " He squeezed her.

Sat next to Angela.

Silence.

Easter drums sounded and the rear doors opened, held by ushers in white.

Four choirs stood. Seniors in black. Gospel in wine. Anthem in green. Youth in white. One hundred and forty voices sang the hymn of Ancient Black Egyptians, Psalms of David:

> Praise ye the Lord
> Praise God in his Sanctuary

> Praise him
> In the firmament of his power.

The drummers answered. Joshua and Kwame, drums trailing the four colors of Ghana. They stood in the doorway and drummed to wake up the dead. Joshua whose arms had grown strong, who was tall, with eyes flashing like his Grandfather Torch, stood with his smaller brother Kwame, eight years, dressed in African cloth. They drummed and drummed. Lit fires felt by the sun.

> Praise him
> For his mighty acts
> Praise him
> According to his excellent greatness.

The drummers stepped, followed by sisters and brothers in a dazzle of African prints. Gold, green and red. Ethiopia's colors. Juma three, Leith four, marched behind the drummers. The church laughing at their smallness. Cymbals. Triangles.

> Praise him
> With the sound of the trumpet.

Nine sisters and brothers. Carried nine horns. Zaria nine years, Bell-Abeba six. They came in twos with mello-phones, trumpets. Trumpets polished with new wool. Valves washed, oiled. Relined and tested.

Choir voices fell through the church. Showered the drummers. The musicians. In songs bright colors of African cloth. Azzisa, eleven. Soft hair bounced around her face. Jared twelve, walked with her. They fought daily. Argued in the dressing room. Walked peacefully now.

Praise him.

Something had been recovered from The Middle Passage. After twenty-five years of birth.

Praise him.

The hundred million lost in the ocean, remembered. Abeba's heart beat with Daniel's heart.

Praise him.
Praise him
With the psaltery and the harp.
Praise him
With the timbrel and dance.

Asa, bushy-haired and lean, carried his long trombone proper at his side. Arthur Lavoisier, named for his step-grandfather, marched. Wide bones in his solid body. His mind sharp with knowledge.

Praise him
Upon the high-sounding cymbals

Little-Angela soft smile in her eyes. Tall. Love heat flushed Abeba. The choir-song showered her Kora. Daniel-Jr. Askia-Touré. Who stopped at the piano and stood while the others gathered their African cloth and mounted the pulpit. Stood still before

Reverend Judges while Joshua and Kwame redoubled their drum-
mings. Ignored the shouts and hollers and drummed, brother
watching brother exploding life.

They were still.

> Let everything that hath breath
> Praise the Lord.
> Praise ye the Lord.

"Praise the Lord," Angela answered.

There was a flurry of commotion as Osei left Angela, scrambled
up the steps and stood next to Daniel-Jr.

"Praise the Lord," Angela called.

Church laughter. Quieted.

Askia-Touré sat next to Abeba. He was a man now. Master of
music. April light fell on his face. New hair growing on his lip and
chin. He was twenty-three. He smiled shyly, echoed Abeba's smile.
Ready.

Horns flashed a solid ring of gold. Abeba nodded and drums
rolled. The children who breathed water in the same womb, who
gathered new songs from tired flesh, brought the overcrowded
years, sickness, madness to this Easter moment. Their spirits gathered around her like bright yellow suns. Their bodies struggled
with the music. Askia's hands stretched. Right hand jumped
through Abeba's hands. He laughed. Turned a quick trill, pretty as
Jupiter's brick-red moon. Landed on the night keys. Music. Made
Jesus answer. Got him to talk.

Abeba nodded. Music dropped. Pianissimo. Quiet . . . pianissimo . . .

"First time I sang at First Baptist, I was just getting over my brother's death."

"Well."

"Felt like I couldn't make it."

"Well."

"But I got a son named Joshua now. That's the big one drumming."

"All right."

"And I don't feel so lonesome anymore."

The church laughed.

"My brothers here to help me sing. To remember Joshua on this day of life . . ."

Against the day they turned the pots down so it wouldn't carry sound of enslaved blacks praying . . . way down yonder.

There was pretty age in their voices. Men-voices filled with brotherly years. Daniel. Matthew. Calvin. Singing against the soft beat of drums. Piano. Horns. Gray hairs colored Matthew's moustache. Their shoulders broader, solid with age . . .

> Seeking Jesus
> Couldn't hear nobody pray.
> Chilly Jordan
> Couldn't hear nobody pray.

Easter flowers glistened. The sun fell through stained glass windows. Light and color covered the Easter church. Silence. Shining edge of horns. Pianissimo. Blue notes. Kora's horn. A spinning trill. Askia answered. Blue note. Arthur-Lavoisier . . . A sun-soft chord Zaria. Abeba answered.

Calvin and Matthew hummed. Sweetly. The church sucked breath as Daniel pulled his head forward, opened his mouth to one side and again the blackest pure bass dropped lower and lower (couldn't hear nobody pray) until the whole Easter church slipped into the low-dark voice and cried out.

22   It was raining. Soft rain. Steady rain. It was a peaceful
         rain filled with many thoughts, good years. Abeba stood
on the sun porch with Kora and Little-Angela watching the rain.
Listening to the rain.

"In North Carolina, I remember the boiled peanuts."

"Boiled peanuts!"

"Jackson Gold used to come by every day. Said he would marry
me when we grew up."

It rained.

"One day I remember fixing such nice mud pies and I guess
they looked so real, so tempting, next thing I heard a crunch."

Rain falling. Quiet, private October morning. The streets empty
of barking dogs. Morning people. Occasionally children in rain-
coats and boots walking to school. The neighbors to work. In the
quiet October rain. Rain falling.

"It was so quiet when Daniel-Jr was born." Daniel at Tallahoochee could barely walk.

The gutter rain beat in splashing sheets, rolled out into the
streets. Calvin's trial thinned Daniel's mind. His brother dying
thinned his mind. She pulled Kora closer. Little-Angela. All these
years they never mentioned that beating.

"After your father sang at our church, Mommie took me to a
palm reader."

"She did!"

"I don't know why all my life, even after the concert, she looks at me. Never smiles." She felt Kora's arm tighter around her. Listened to the rain falling, soft rain and gentle rain. Even where it rushed from the gutter and rolled out into the streets, somehow quiet and peaceful. Rain. Rain.

"You should have heard your father singing that August afternoon."

Kora smiled. Little-Angela. Listening to the rain.

Daniel would be fifty in five days. Abeba had watched the gray hairs fill his beard. In the first morning light she saw the stiff gray hairs sprinkled like fine cereal on his face and chin. Thick hair began to thin in the center of his head, space the size of a dime spread to a quarter. Moments ago she stood at the door, touched his coat collar, kissed him. Watched until he slipped around the corner. Like time slipping out of sight. So much time had vanished. Where did it go? In the rain falling, soft and steady rain this last Monday in October. Time. Was in Azzisa's hair, thick and soft. In Zaria's bright eyes. Queenly walk. Kwame's drumming. Bell's bounce, bright laugh. Leith's melancholy eyes. Time was in Juma's love for his brother. If she had time to write a book she would write about Juma, two years old and looking out for his brother. Osei. Kora said he had waited twenty-five years in the womb. A shadow who watched fourteen sisters and brothers form, and finally, twenty-five years later, came ruddy-skinned. Big-framed. At the tip of his widow's peak, one purely white hair. Symbol of age. The womb had to go after that. Clipped out, fibrous and bleeding.

Rain fell, and Abeba tightened her arm around Kora. Who looked like her father. Plump lips, black and Indian smooth. Slim face. Her partner. Twenty years old. They talked about Carolina. St. Augustine. Mamma Habblesham and Jackson Gold. If she was forty-five, he must be about sixty! She kept thinking of him as fifteen. Sixteen.

"Mamma," Kora said. "Did you hear what Osei said?"

"What did he say?"

"He spoke in German."

"German?"

"He heard Asa and Joshua practicing."

"That boy!"

Listened to the rain.

Last week, she noticed it. Just a faint yellow color in the eye when she pulled the lid down, deeper yellow. She would check it. After Daniel's birthday celebration. They might have damaged something during the last operation.

"Mamma!" Azzisa called from the kitchen.

"I know this peace wouldn't last long. What is it, Azzisa?"

They went to the kitchen.

"I hate farina."

"What's that, child?"

"I said I hate farina."

"My goodness. Such strong feeling against a bowl of cereal. Please, Azzisa, don't start any new foolishness today."

"Oh, it ain't new. I always hated . . ."

"Sit down and slide that little cereal on down. And don't comb your hair into your eyes."

"Stop trying to be sexy," Jared said.

"Jared, you let me talk."

"That's right, blubber lip."

"You heard that, Mamma? Heard that idiot Azzisa making fun of the way God made my mouth?"

She sighed. "Son. I should have stayed out of the kitchen. You were doing all right until I stepped in. Son, why can't you avoid that word. You're not a doctor. Idiot is a medical term."

"She was talking about my mouth."

"Eat, son."

"I can't stand this stuff blobbed out on the plate so lifeless and gooey," Azzisa said. "And I don't care about the people in India, Africa even eating black bean soup and black bread to match."

"Azzisa!"

"Is there such a thing as black bean soup?"

"Yes, Leith."

"And black bread?"

"Yes, Leith."

"I hope it's not dirty." Leith chewed and thought. Four years old. They called to her, but Abeba's mind was with the rain.

"Guess what Kwame brought Papa for his birthday?" Jared asked. Then said, "Peanut brittle. Sophie Mae."

They laughed. They all laughed, including Juma, three years old, who was Harriet Tubman this morning and sat at the table holding a towel around his head.

"He opened the box and ate some, then scotchtaped it closed. He—he tried to get me to eat some too so he wouldn't feel so guilty."

"Jared, Jared. Where is your brother? Don't come to the table satisfied to pack your stomach tight . . ."

"My stomach ain't tight."

"All right. I'm through talking."

"Go ahead, Mamma. I'm listening."

"It's already after eight. Call your brother to breakfast."

"That stupid idiot." Jared took a noisy slurp of milk. Wiped a trickle from his chin. "Kwame knows it's time for breakfast." He stood and shouted. "Get down here Kwame before I have to bring you down. Nut!"

"Son, don't act illiterate, yelling right in your mother's ear."

"He knows it's time for breakfast, though."

She heard her children through her thoughts. Through the rain. Fast and silent rain. It splashed sky-colored. Its shy gray filled the yard. She heard the clink of spoon on teeth, plate. Deep slurps of milk. A voice ask for sugar. Sugar lifted in soft-peaked piles, quiet against the rain falling. October. October raining.

Abeba, Little-Angela, Kora, back on the sun porch. Watched the rain falling.

23　　After Abeba looked in the mirror and her eyes stared back at her yellow, wolf's eyes, that was it. Time for the general hospital. It was bile spilled in her system. Something wrong with the gall bladder. They tested her blood, found sugar. She didn't eat much sugar. Gave her a special diet, medicine. Sent her home. She came back and they kept her.

Abeba saw the nurses come eternally to take blood. Pressure. More blood. More pressure. They turned her over, lifted her gown and gave her needles in the buttocks. Brought pills in paper cups. Tiny cups of water. The general hospital was crowded. In this room marked Solitary, seventeen beds. They gave one woman a sock for a washcloth.

The third time she saw that troop of nurses in hats like starched wings roll that jangling cart to her bed, Abeba lifted her head.

"I've had all my blood tests," she said. But they took more blood. For bilirubin. Went off. They put her on a complete fast, strapped her naked to a table, swung her upside down. She was cold. Blood rushed to her head, made her eyes bulge. She thought she was falling. X-rayed her body. The table straps digging into her shoulders holding her. Even now her shoulders were sore.

A lady came close to her bed. "You better eat today, so you get well and see those children." She pointed in Abeba's face. Climbed into her own bed. She meant well. But she was an ignorant woman who did a lot of talking. Never listened.

Abeba's thoughts stopped. Someone was smoking in bed. She propped herself. She couldn't afford to start wheezing. Not while she had yellow eyes. One thing at a time.

"Dolores, that you smoking?"

"I'm almost finished."

"Please smoke that in the bathroom."

Dolores got up. Grufty-haired. Dolores cussed regularly every night. Hollered for the nurse.

Abeba lay back. Thinking of home. Daniel bought a tall tree. Said the top bent against the ceiling. The children decorated it. Drenched in silver. Delicate bulbs. She said I'll be home for Christmas. Tomorrow was Christmas. She would not be home.

All Christmas Day, from early morning, the public hospital was a nest of noise. Visitors came in coats trailing cold wind. Brought cards and presents. Angela came.

"Merry Christmas. Merry Christmas."

Everyone knew her.

"Merry Christmas."

Abeba prepared herself.

Angela sat at the bed. Wordless. Took out oranges. Apples. Bananas. Put them on the little table. Small box of candy.

"You stay sick. So full of ache and pain. This hurt. That hurt. Got more ache and pain than a old woman." She looked Abeba full in the face. "You not going to get up from this bed. You going to die right here."

"Nurse!" Abeba called across to Dolores. "Call the nurse."

"Nurse!" Dolores broke eardrums. Two nurses came running.

"Take my mother out of here."

"I borned you."

"Take her away."

The PA system called for Dr. Beezeemer. As if answering a cue, a troop of doctors in wrinkly green clothes rolled in. Green caps, green smocks, green pants, green shoes. Pulled the curtain where a woman slept. Big-faced woman. Deep black skin. Covered and rolled out. The bed stripped.

Abeba watched them roll her away. Dead.

Sounds burst sharp against her jangled nerves. She had always gone home. How many hospitals had she known since her father died. Childbirths. Operations. Asthma.

She looked up and saw her Daniel quick-stepping.

She would go home again.

24 Abeba Williams Lavoisier Torch. August. Her mind had been pulled out to a place where there was no tree. Her eyes large in her face. Big knees topped her skinny legs. Her body jarred as she walked, fat gone from the balls of her feet. She made it home. The recruiting officer dressed in brown had come for three sons. The Long Island sky filled with silver planes. War again. Sometimes she was in the floating zone where silence is solid stone. Mrs. Torch.

She heard the children laughing outside and struggled up. Took her slow-stepping-dangling-walk to the door. Looked out.

"Osei can swim," Bell shouted. Ran from the water, dripping, feet soft on the dirt, then thap-thap thapping on the pavement. Bell blazed life. Smiled and spoke more softly now that she was close. "Osei was swimming, no kidding. Pretty good for somebody two years old." She hugged Abeba. Ran back. She had a pretty, wide nose. Hair that flamed red at the edges. Broad shoulders. Pretty, strong legs.

"Mamma!"

"Mamma!"

The others called to her.

Abeba waved.

She had to leave Daniel now. After twenty-six years. St. Augustine. Maryland. Brooklyn. Built the bakery. Bought this house. Wanted her to travel. See African nations.

Her thin finger traced the ridge of the incision. Midway between the breasts to the bottom of her belly. Body cut open and closed. Laced with baseball stitches. Even while heat in her body burned like hell's suns, she said, let me go home. They said the pain will get worse. The vital organs disintegrate.

She came home. Blood had flowed for her in the neighborhood. For all the operations. She was ashamed to come home so thin. But cancer eats in a hurry. She cried at night. Tears fell in the facial hollows. Rolled down fevered bones.

"Beba?"

"I'm at the back, Daniel." She answered quickly. So he wouldn't think she was gone. He cried a deep, frightening cry.

"There you are."

He helped her down the steps. Into a soft chair. They sat under the arbor. Watched the children. She wanted to live. See the children. Osei, Juma, Leith, Bell-Abeba grow into tall men and women. Zaria at nine, writing such beautiful lines. "The morning ka-ploshed into my face. Filled with God's love." Daniel-Jr, Askia-Touré. The big children would soon have children. She would like to visit Africa. But the grass . . . brown and patched in so many places. There had been no rain. The last days held massive pain.

"Well, Daniel." She was quiet now. God has plans which mortals don't understand. He rests in the womb when the new baby forms. Whispers the life-dream to infinitesimal cells. It is God who lies under the thoughts of man. He is cartilage. Memory. The spinning of this earth and a thousand other earths. Sound. Distance. God forms our blue songs. Creates the stammering tongue and leaves motherless children crying. It is God in the house when the curtains lift gently at windows and a young child sucks her itching gums. We do not understand the mysteries of God. God the winter. Summer. Septembers. Moody dark tones of fathers dying. The splash and laughter. Children playing. She had screamed at God two weeks ago.

Her mind was quiet now. Thin hand squeezed Daniel's arm. "My husband. My best friend." She sighed. "It's time."

25 The blue grapes were fat on the arbor. Under leaves silver green, all sparking after the night's heavy rain. A frightening rain. A strong wind shook the house, rattled every window, and the Torch children awoke, moved from room to room. Talked about their mother. When morning came, it was a brilliant, quiet Saturday. August. The mother dead. Squirrels hopped across the bright wet grass. Rainwater filled the pool. The children's playthings, swings, slides still wet. Outside it was still summer, bright and glowing.

Inside, the neighbors gathered, spoke with relatives. Wore black. Sat in quick-quiet conversation. Voices hushed.

"You see all that bread Daniel baked?"

"He sure taking it hard, isn't he?"

"Naturally."

"Look like just when he get to the place where he see light of day, this tragedy happen."

"Isn't it so."

Voice lower. "You see how Osei holds Daniel's shirt tail?"

Yolanda opened her pocketbook.

The others watched from the corner of an eye as she blew her nose. They saw tears through her dark glasses.

"Now, Osei is a baby, isn't he?"

"Just turned two."

"Osei?" Grandmother Torch called him. "Come sit with Grandmother."

He came and sat on her lap. She patted his knees and brushed his legs.

Matthew watched. His eyes red. He had liquor on his breath. "Don't you think somebody ought to tell Daniel it's time? He ain't dressed yet."

Calvin went to the kitchen. Surveyed the tables filled with bread and cake. There was enough bread to feed the world. "I think you have enough here," Calvin said.

"Yeah. I think I got enough cakes. Bread."

"Yes. You have enough." He hesitated. "It's almost eleven o'clock, you'd better dress now."

"Won't take me long to dress." He did a few more things while Calvin watched anxiously.

Then he suddenly walked through the living room, walked quickly.

Osei scrambled from Grandmother Torch's lap and ran after his father. Grabbed his shirt tail.

"Osei?" Aunt Loretta called him.

Askia-Touré walked through red-eyed. His piano partner was dead.

"Askia."

"How you doing, Askia?"

Joshua. The drummer. Broad-shouldered. Tall like Papa Torch who died five years ago. Daniel-Jr. Big sons who filled the room. They went out to the sun porch to wait.

Kora's voice filtered down the steps. Leith and Bell-Abeba came into the living room dressed in white. Little-Angela, dressed in black.

"Here are my granddaughters," Mamma Torch said.

"How come everybody's wearing black dresses? Me and Bell's wearing white dresses?" Leith looked around. "Is Mamma coming home today?"

Neighbors gathered at the door and waited until Daniel came downstairs. Dressed. Looking slim and alone. "I'm about as ready as I'll ever be," he said.

Four cars rolled into Harlem. One Hundred and Thirty-seventh Street filled with commotion. Car doors opened. People watched the Torches enter that dark place of waiting people, flowers and prayer. Where time bent and broke one African Flower. It seemed an eternity before the lavender casket had been opened and closed. The last impression of Abeba in white organdy dress, face powdered. Lips clamped shut.

As the mourners stepped onto the sidewalk, out in the sun again, Daniel bellowed the pain of the mad. Loretta threw her arms around him and Mamma Torch screamed, "Jesus! Give them back their mother." The Torch children who agreed not to cry until they got home, cried.

They didn't know that four days ago, at three in the morning, an old midwife had slipped into Abeba's room, had taken her hand and gone up the hill. The noon bell rang that Saturday in August. The old woman listened. She studied the nine sons, six daughters. Daniel-Jr, Askia-Touré, Kora, Joshua, Asa, Little-Angela, Arthur-Lavoisier, Jared, Azzisa, Zaria, Kwame, Bell-Abeba, Leith, Juma, Osei. She studied the husband in the sister's arms, weeping. Saw the lavender casket carried to the car. Grandma Hattie, Ohio, crying. Heard Angela's loud voice calling, "Sleep on. Sleep on."

And the midwife said ever so quietly, "Hush your mouth."

And the lion shall eat straw like the ox.

Reading Group Guide for *Let the Lion Eat Straw*

A Novel by Ellease Southerland

Introduction

Six-year-old Abeba has been raised by Mamma Habblesham, a woman whose love for the child is boundless. But when her birth mother returns to North Carolina to claim the child she left behind, it changes the course of Abeba's life. Leaving behind the poverty and despair of the rural South, she heads north to begin a new life in Brooklyn.

Happiness and tragedy alternately define Abeba's childhood, from the joy of excelling in school to the death of her beloved stepfather. Through it all, her exceptional musical talent promises to be an avenue of escape—not just for her, but for her mother, who is intent on seeing Abeba become a concert pianist.

When Daniel, a handsome young singer, enters Abeba's life, her musical career is set aside for marriage and motherhood. As she and Daniel build a life together, raise their children, and weather challenges, Abeba finds that even as some dreams fade, others rise to take their place.

Ellease Southerland, Maya Angelou has said, "is a seer of the interior landscape," and in *Let the Lion Eat Straw* she captures the extraordinary in seemingly ordinary lives. This is a tale of family and forgiveness, sorrow and resilience. Above all, it's the story of a woman living her life with quiet grace and dignity. Like the sounds of Abeba's music, *Let the Lion Eat Straw* will resonate in your heart and mind long after you turn the last page.

Discussion Questions

1. Why do you suppose the author chose "Let the Lion Eat Straw" as the title? Is there any significance to its being a passage from the Bible?

2. *Let the Lion Eat Straw* was first published more than twenty-five years ago and is set in the earlier part of the twentieth century. Are there timeless aspects of the story that you can relate to? What are they?

3. Why did Angela return for Abeba six years after leaving her in the care of Mamma Habblesham? Angela viewed her daughter as "not a little girl, but trouble, trouble." Did she really want her daughter to come live with her in Brooklyn?

4. Abeba never sees Mamma Habblesham again after she leaves North Carolina, but does the midwife remain a presence in her life? Discuss the references to Mamma Habblesham throughout the story, including the ending.

5. Why does Angela repeatedly say to Abeba, "I borned you?" How would you describe Abeba's relationship with Angela?

6. Abeba initially sees Daniel at the First Baptist Church, where he sings a hymn while she plays for the congregation. What is it about Daniel that attracts Abeba to him and ultimately makes her want to marry him?

7. How does the time Abeba spends in Florida with Daniel's family alter her life and her marriage? How does it most differ from living in Brooklyn?

8. When Angela finds out Abeba is pregnant with her first baby, she warns her not to have any more children or she will tell Daniel about Abeba and Uncle CJ. Did Angela know from the start that CJ was abusing Abeba? If so, why didn't she do anything to stop it?

9. What makes Abeba decide to tell Daniel about the abuse she suffered at the hands of Uncle CJ? Why does she ask Daniel's forgiveness? What was Daniel's reaction when Abeba confides in him?

10. What part does music play in the story? What does it represent to the different characters? Even after Abeba gives up her dream of attending Juilliard, how does she make music a part of her life and the lives of her children?

11. What does chapter 24 reveal about Abeba and Daniel's marriage? Does Abeba regret the path she took in life? Do you think she would change anything if she could?

12. One reviewer said about Let the Lion Eat Straw, "There is more life and character, more that will linger in the mind, than in countless novels twice as long." What lingers most in your mind about Let the Lion Eat Straw?

EBELE OSEYE/ELLEASE SOUTHERLAND, born in New York, is the Gwendolyn Brooks Award winner for poetry and recipient of the Ann Ramsey Award for Scholarly Initiative and Action. She is contributing editor to *Okike: An African Journal of New Writing* and Professor of African literature and creative writing at Pace University, New York. She is the author of *The Magic Sun Spins: Poetry, A Feast of Fools: A Novel, Opening Line: The Creative Writer,* and *This Year in Nigeria: A Memoir.* A forthcoming title includes the poetry collection "A Silver Hieroglyph."

An Interview with Ebele Oseye/Ellease Southerland

In 2004 you celebrated the twenty-fifth anniversary of the book's publication. What was it like to see the book back in print?
I don't know. It was in print for quite a number of years with several foreign editions. And I also restored the book to print in 2000.

What have you been doing both professionally and personally since the book was published?
My professional activities include writing and teaching. My writings include literary essays as well as creative works. I have lectured at public schools and colleges, including the University of Nigeria at Nsukka. I've had some radio and television appearances. I have just contributed poetry recordings to *B.Ma: The Sonia Sanchez Literary Review*, scheduled for fall 2004 publication.

My personal activities include travel to Egypt, Ghana, and Nigeria. I also enjoy baking, reading astronomy, history, the dictionary, nutrition, exercising, dancing, playing the piano when I can snatch a few hours, and enjoying the company of family and friends.

When did you change your name? What was behind your decision to do so?
I changed my name in 1996. It's natural and important for people to have names that resemble them. My great-grandfather Thomas Southerland recently described to me by my oldest uncle, was an unusually strong man and because of his strength, was worked to death by an American slaver. My great-grandfather died young and had only one child, my grandfather. I didn't want to carry the slaver's name to my death. Watching Alex Haley's *Roots* and seeing the horrific whipping Kunta Kinte received in effort to "beat his name out of him" only reinforced my thinking. My parents had already given African names to my youngest siblings, so this was a natural change.

What's the one thing you hope any reader will take away from your novel?
The one thing which I hope a reader will take away from *Let the Lion Eat Straw* is deep regard and deeper appreciation for life.

What inspired you to write *Let the Lion Eat Straw*?
My mother's life is the inspiration for this book. In 1964 my mother and I had an opportunity to meet Ralph Ellison—at a Queens College Ceremony, where I shared first prize for fiction—and he not only reminded us that we should read, but that we must first write about ourselves. His novel and his words encouraged my direction.

What are some of your favorite books and authors?
My favorite authors include:
Gwendolyn Brooks, *Selected Poems*
Zora Neale Hurston, *Their Eyes Were Watching God*
Randall Robinson, *The Debt*
Charles S. Ogletree, Jr. *All Deliberate Speed*
Langston Hughes, *The Best of Simple*
Maya Angelou, *The Heart of a Woman*
Sterling A. Brown, *The Collected Poems*
Alice Childress, *The Wedding Band*
Marita Golden, *Long Distance Life*
Edwidge Danticat, *The Dew Breaker*
Ousmane Sembene, *God's Bits of Wood*
Chinua Achebe, *Morning Yet on Creation Day*
W. E. B. Du Bois, *The Souls of Black Folk*
Paule Marshall, *The Chosen Place, the Timeless People*
Toni Morrison, *Jazz*
James Weldon Johnson, *Along This Way*
James Alan McPherson, *Elbow Room*
Charles Johnson, *Dreamer*
Audre Lorde, *The Black Unicorn*
Joseph Campbell, *Hero of a Thousand Faces*
Molefi K. Asante, *Kemet, Afrocentricity and Knowledge*
Vincent Harding, *There Is a River*
The Papyrus of Ani, ancient Egyptian text
and many others.

Which writers have influenced your work?
All, especially the ancient writers from Kemet (Egypt). The imagery of Thomas Mann and the poetry of Shakespeare also influenced my writing. The honesty and craft of Maya Angelou, the ancestral memory of Zora Neale Hurston, the precision of Gwendolyn Brooks, the daring of

Ralph Ellison and the passion of James Baldwin and the robust characterization of Ousmane Sembene also had a direct influence on my writing.

You wrote this book at a time when many African Americans were leaving their Southern homes for opportunities in the North, just as Abeba's mother did. What thoughts do you have on the current phenomena of reverse migration—young African Americans leaving northern cities for opportunities in the South? Atlanta, for instance, is now referred to as the Black Mecca.
It is good for people to find a place which gives their hearts comfort. The South in certain ways resembles the African village. People care more about people. There is home cooking and a closer connection to nature. A number of my closest friends have recently relocated to Georgia, some to Atlanta. There are still many people migrating to New York.

How and why do you split your time between the United States and Nigeria?
I live and work in New York. I have been spending my summers in Nigeria, where I have been renting a house for the past seven years. I enjoy the people, the language, and the culture (I'm always having misunderstandings since English is used in different ways and this keeps my sense of humor alive!). I most of all appreciate an opportunity to return to African soil and to have a closer connection to African culture, despite the hellish intentions of the Middle Passage.

Upon publication, the *New Yorker* said your book read like a myth: "Ellease Southerland's own dreams and memories, as well as her literary style, are imbued with African folklore, making her story seem less a novel than a myth." Are you inspired by mythology?
Yes. I am very much inspired by mythology, including the first fratricide on record, the murder of Osiris at the hands of his brother, Set, more than forty-five hundred years ago. Myth helps us to transcend brutality and death. Myth returns the hope, the wonder, and surprise essential for life.